THE
FRANKLIN
AFFAIR

THE
FRANKLIN
AFFAIR

A NOVEL

JIM LEHRER

RANDOM HOUSE TRADE PAPERBACKS   *New York*

2006 Random House Trade Paperback Edition

Published in the United States by Random House Trade Paperbacks, an imprint of The Random House Publishing Group, a division of Random House, Inc., New York.

RANDOM HOUSE TRADE PAPERBACKS and colophon are registered trademarks of Random House, Inc.

Originally published in hardcover in the United States by Random House, an imprint of The Random House Publishing Group, a division of Random House, Inc., in 2005.

LIBRARY OF CONGRESS CATALOGING-IN-PUBLICATION DATA

Lehrer, James.
  The Franklin affair: a novel / Jim Lehrer.
    p.   cm.
  ISBN 0-345-46803-1
  1. Biographers—Fiction. 2. Philadelphia (Pa.)—Fiction. 3. Franklin, Benjamin, 1706–1790—Fiction. 4. Funeral rites and ceremonies—Fiction. 5. Extortion—Fiction. I. Title.
  PS3562.E4419F35 2005   813'.54—dc22   2004051347

Printed in the United States of America

www.atrandom.com

9 8 7 6 5 4 3 2

Design by Mauna Eichner

Always, for Kate

No false move should ever be made to

extricate yourself out of a difficulty,

or to gain an advantage.

—BENJAMIN FRANKLIN,
The Morals of Chess

THE
FRANKLIN
AFFAIR

ONE

Rebecca Kendall Lee, on the attack, made an obvious point of staring at Reginald Raymond Taylor.

"Less than five percent of the aphorisms in the almanacs of your own great Ben Franklin were original," she said. "The rest were filched—plagiarized—in meaning if not words, isn't that right, R?"

"R" had long ago become Taylor's preferred way to be addressed because he detested both of his given names.

More important at this moment, he detested Rebecca.

She stood at her place at a table in a room at the Cosmos Club, a private club in Washington, for this early morning confrontation with R and three other historians of the American Revolution. They were looking into formal accusations against her that had arisen from the recent rumble of newspaper reports on alleged plagiarism and other crimes of creation by some popular writers of American history.

R successfully fought off any automatic reaction to her almanac claim. He didn't smile or frown, shift his head, or move an eye, an eyebrow, or any other part of his body. He also didn't repeat the fact, definitely known to Rebecca, that Franklin openly admitted to taking most of what appeared in the almanacs from other sources. He just assembled and printed.

Rebecca raised her gaze from R to the others and declared, "So who really knows who takes what from whom? Let any of *you* or—to borrow a bit from Tennessee Williams's *Cat*—any reporters of the *Los Angeles Times, The New York Times,* or any other damned *Times* who has not snatched an idea, a thought, or a form of words cast the first stone."

Her defiance was reinforced naturally by her physical presence. Rebecca, who was in her late thirties, was at least five feet ten inches tall and large-boned—almost husky—and wore her long black hair hanging down her back like an Indian warrior in a 1950s movie, a look that had also helped make her a forceful television personality. She was a former colleague of R's who had, in fact, begun her career with a small book on the hundreds of sayings in Ben's many editions of *Poor Richard's Almanack.* She moved on to be a Ronald Reagan historian and conservative TV political commentator.

R had hoped that Rebecca had demanded to appear before this special committee of the American Revolution Historical Association as a prelude to her accepting some kind of quiet sanction. He should have known better.

When no one responded to her, she added, "I hereby challenge each and every one of you who dares sit in judgment of me to rise now before the God of Benjamin Franklin, Poor Richard, or any other person or event of American revolutionary history and swear you have not also similarly sinned."

R did not rise and swear to anything. Neither did the other three. Only once had they stood, and that was to begin the meeting with a quick toast—sherry, tea, and coffee were available on the table—to the memory of Wallace Stephen Rush, who had died the night before in Philadelphia. Wally Rush was one of America's leading Franklin scholars, as well as R's great friend and mentor.

"If you are waiting for our tearful confessions, Dr. Lee, I suspect you wait in vain," said John Gwinnett, the chairman, breaking the silence of the committee. "This is not a television program, so I suggest you be seated, so we can go about this unpleasant business in an orderly and efficient manner—and so our colleague, Dr. Taylor, can be on his way to Philadelphia."

Gwinnett was a distinguished professor of history at William and Mary who specialized in Patrick Henry. He was in his mid-seventies, and with his flowing white hair, half-glasses down on his nose, and pure Virginia-gentry accent he was a perfect portrait of an American Revolution historian. His chop at Rebecca about television was consistent with his remarks during a panel discussion at last year's ARHA annual convention in Boston. He said that serious historians speaking on television about subjects beyond their specialties was "a cheapening, demeaning, indefensible selling of one's professional credentials that was comparable to whoring." But another panelist, a young author of a Pulitzer Prize–winning book on the Boston Tea Party who appeared often on television, had responded, "I thinketh the distinguished professor overstates from a position of neglect—and, dare I suggest, jealousy? Maybe if he studied a historical subject that provided insights into the present-day world or was prepared to relate stories of drama or interest, maybe an MSNBC, Fox, or CNN booker would beckon him to appear also. TV Booker Envy is a terrible thing to see in a colleague so distinguished—and so senior."

Rebecca ignored Gwinnett's TV comment now. There were clearly more important matters on the table. "I am interested in neither order nor efficiency—not even for R's and Wally's sakes," she said to Gwinnett. "My only interest is in justice."

She moved her dark-brown eyes slowly from Gwinnett to each of the other faces at the table. But then she did sit down.

The faces besides Gwinnett's and R's belonged to Sonya Lyman and Joseph Arthur Hooper. Sonya was a prominent Adams Family Dynasty scholar at Harvard who was a Rebecca opposite in most matters except gender, race, profession, and age. They were both active in a group of women historians, but that was it for compatibility. Sonya was small, unobtrusive, and unassuming. Her hair was beige, straight, and short. Her politics were left, academic, quiet.

Joe Hooper was a fifty-five-year-old light-skinned black man with a beard who taught economic history at Brown and had written extensively on the Founding Fathers' attitudes toward slavery. His best-known book, *The Founding Racists,* was mostly an excoriation of Washington, Jefferson, and Madison for their ownership of slaves, but it also contained a grudging tribute to Franklin, whom Hooper labeled "our first abolitionist" for his antislavery leadership *after* the Revolution.

"We are here today, Dr. Lee, because you asked for a meeting," said Gwinnett. "We have only begun to assemble the material that will help us resolve the professional and ethical questions that have been raised about your work—most particularly in *Ronald Reagan: The Last Founding Father,* your 457-page survey of Ronald Reagan's miracles and achievements, done in an eighteenth-century context—"

Rebecca interrupted, her eyes shining. "Book. It's a book. I wrote a book, not a survey. Surveys are taken by telemarketers who ask questions over the phone about shampoo preferences and magazine subscriptions. I spent eighteen months of hard work and thought on that book."

Eighteen months! thought R. And she thinks that constitutes hard work and thought? She knows full well that Wally Rush spent most of his adult life getting into the head and being of Benjamin

Franklin. Until recently, R himself had worked on little else in his career apart from Ben, as had many others.

"I stand corrected," said Gwinnett, who, R knew, had labored for at least thirty-five years on Patrick Henry. "It's a book that appeared under your name."

"I wrote it!" Rebecca said. Her voice rose in intensity and volume to match the loathing in those two brown eyes.

"That, of course, is one of the issues now before us," said Gwinnett. Clearly, if Rebecca thought she was going to roll John Gwinnett, she thought wrong. However, R felt the old professor was being unnecessarily provocative. There was no need to insult her so directly and so snidely.

Rebecca raised her two hands over her head in surrender.

She looked at R. "So, it's welcome to the railroading—I could say lynching—of Rebecca Kendall Lee, is that it, R?"

R loathed it when people referred to themselves in the third person, but he put a friendly smile on his face and said, "Innocent until proven guilty lies at the heart of the system created by our beloved Founding Fathers, Rebecca. That concept will guide this committee, I guarantee it."

"Me too," said Joe Hooper. "I didn't volunteer and I agreed reluctantly when chosen to perform this duty, Dr. Lee, but I can assure you that I will look at the evidence and arrive at a decision in a fair and unbiased manner. There will be no lynching. They are over—for historians as well as for black people."

R didn't know Joe Hooper very well personally and had not seen him in action before. He was clearly solid—and smart. R had wrongly assumed that Hooper was on this committee solely because the ARHA leadership saw a need for diversity—for a non-Caucasian face. That, of course, would run counter to the association's claim that all four had been selected at random from a bowl that contained the names of the entire membership of seventeen-hundred-plus professional historians.

Now only John Gwinnett and Sonya Lyman were left to declare themselves as fair-minded decent human beings who would not be party to a railroading or lynching of Rebecca Kendall Lee.

It was obvious in a heartbeat that John was going to take a pass on any such declaration. He was clearly not about to make some kind of defensive statement about his ability to run a professional inquiry. His integrity went without saying.

R had to suppress a whoop at the sight of Rebecca and Sonya doing a ten-count dance of glances and stares. Finally, Rebecca aimed her brown lasers right at Sonya's face, which was turned downward at the table at some doodling she was doing on a notepad. R was unable to see what Sonya was drawing, but he wouldn't have been surprised if it was a stick figure of Rebecca hanging by her neck from a tree limb. The hostility over politics and style between these two women was well-known. Sonya had once referred to Rebecca at small gathering of women historians as a "right-wing witch." Rebecca, upon hearing this, was said to have responded, "I'm a moderate in everything but politics."

Sonya neither raised her head nor said a word now. Rebecca also said nothing.

"Unless you have some specific point you would like to raise, we might as well conclude this meeting," said Gwinnett to Rebecca. "We will contact you for direct comment once we have done our basic research."

Rebecca took a deep here-goes breath and looked down as if praying or vowing or collecting her thoughts—possibly all three.

The small room was as silent as it had been since the five professional American historians gathered in it less than an hour ago.

R raised a hand to get Gwinnett's nod to speak.

"Rebecca, could you give us a rough idea of what we're likely to find in the research?" he said. "Are there in fact misappropriated phrases, passages, and whatever in your Reagan book?"

"At this point I plead guilty to nothing," said Rebecca. "I can't, of course, rule out the possibility of some zealous detective of yours isolating a questionable line or two—but there would be less than a handful and much, *much* less than the ninety-five percent in Ben's work."

"I trust that 'Everybody does it' is not your own defense," R said, and then immediately wished to hell he hadn't. There are occasions when silence is the perfect response. This was one of those—now missed—times.

"In fact, R, I do have one more thing to say to all of you along those lines," said Rebecca, now in full fighting mode. She pushed her chair back from the table and stood. Oration and intimidation time had come again.

"Please be forewarned, each and every one of you, my most distinguished colleagues, that yours will not be the only investigation being conducted. Earlier today I made a formal request to the women historians' organization, of which Sonya is also a member, to assemble a group of researchers to peruse the work of each of you. If they won't do it, I will. Either way, every word you have individually written in books, articles, and papers, as well as said in speeches and interviews—even in the classroom—will be checked. I call it Operation First Stone. If this comes down to a public fight, rest assured it will not be one-sided."

This time there was the perfect rejoinder: Nobody said a word.

"I trust I will see all of you in Philadelphia at Wally Rush's funeral—memorial service—whatever," said Rebecca at the meeting-room door. Looking at R she added, "It will be on the twenty-first of April, as was Ben's?"

R nodded in the affirmative.

"Has the time, place, and form been set?"

R shook his head. "That will be worked out later today."

"Whenever, it will surely be a major gathering of our hallowed trade—most particularly the Crowd," said Rebecca.

She meant the Ben Crowd. That was what Benjamin Franklin scholars were often called. Wally Rush had been their informal leader.

That thought could have triggered Rebecca's departing hit. "As a matter of passing and most relevant fact, R, there were some of us lowly grad students around at the time who questioned whether Wally, may he rest in peace, really wrote all of *Ben Two*."

R remained absolutely still. *Ben Two* was the second volume of Wally's premier Franklin biography. It had won the Pulitzer Prize.

Moments after she was gone and the door closed behind her, Gwinnett said, "In response to Dr. Lee's insanities and threats, I have only to say—borrowing a phrase from Franklin Roosevelt—'We have nothing to fear but fear itself.' "

There were sighs and smiles and shrugs from Joe Hooper and Sonya Lyman but no words. R couldn't get a read on whether fear was indeed all they had to fear.

One could have well been thinking, *I have only to say—to borrow a phrase from Priscilla Alden—"Speak for yourself, John."*

As they got up to go, Gwinnett, Hooper, and Sonya confirmed to R that each would definitely be in Philadelphia on the twenty-first to pay their respects to Wally Rush.

"Meanwhile," said Gwinnett, "an independent research firm retained by the ARHA has almost completed its check of Dr. Lee's Reagan book. The results—the goods, shall we call them—will be dispatched quickly to each of you. I am about to have a right-knee replacement operation, but I would think we should be able to resolve this by conference call in relatively short order."

All this seemed to R to be going awfully fast. But quicker really was better if "the goods" were, in fact, the goods and not, as Rebecca claimed, fewer than a handful of examples.

TWO

Wally Rush had left no doubt about what he wanted done with his body and the other remains of his distinguished life. But by the time R arrived in Philadelphia, there was already talk of ignoring the old man's major wish concerning his funeral.

"No public service?" said Elbridge Clymer, Benjamin Franklin University's young president. "That's ridiculous."

"Ridiculous or not," said Bill Paine, Wally's lawyer and legal executor, "he was most firm on not wanting either a public funeral or a memorial service."

This give-and-take was happening among several of Wally's best friends. They were sitting in eighteenth-century chairs around a corner coffee table amid the high ceilings and bookshelves of the library in the president's house on the campus of BFU, one of the many Philadelphia institutions that had founding ties to Ben Franklin.

"There must be a celebration of the largest and most generous proportions that suits his place as America's leading authority on Benjamin Franklin and one of our institution's most distinguished and honored presences," said Clymer.

"The only real celebration he wants is a full-dress viewing at Gray House the night after his death—tonight—for invited guests only," said Paine. He was a sixtyish, steady, white shirt/wine-tie liberal Republican who handled legal matters for Wally as well as most everything historically civic in Philadelphia.

"I say, on behalf of his great university, request denied," Clymer declared.

Forty-three and known for his energy and his crew cut, Clymer was a BFU alum who had returned as president two years ago after teaching computer mathematics and serving as provost at Lafayette, Chicago, and Princeton.

Paine added, "Wally's only other specific request was that his body be cremated and his ashes tossed to the winds in a small private fashion at Christ Church Burial Ground four days later—on the twenty-first, of course."

Of course. Wally had died yesterday, April 17, in his bed on Settlement Street at the age of eighty-four. Ben, also eighty-four, had died in his bed on April 17, 1790, a few blocks away on Market Street. Ben was buried on April 21 at Christ Church Burial Ground.

R knew the coincidences were no accidents.

Wally, suffering for the last eighteen months from an untreatable liver disease, had often spoken of his intention to time the day of his death to coincide with Ben's. "Jefferson and Adams pulled it off on the exact same day in the same year, which is not possible in my case, obviously, but I may be able to do something in that vein," he had said, referring to the remarkable fact that Thomas Jefferson and John Adams both died of natural causes within hours of each other on July 4, 1826, at their respectives homes: Adams in Quincy, Massachusetts; Jefferson at Monticello outside Charlottesville, Virginia.

R could only guess what unnatural assistance Wally used to make the April 17 timing work for him.

Paine said there might be a problem with the burial ground people on the ashes toss, but he was already talking with them about a compromise. "If we keep it small and private, I'm sure we can work it out."

"No, no, no," said Clymer. "Sorry, Bill, but no small and private."

Bill Paine now said, "R knows—knew—Wally as well if not better than most of us. He can certainly vouch for the fact that when Wally wanted something, particularly when related to Ben, he was adamant."

R nodded, to vouch for Bill Paine's assertion about Wally's adamancy.

Paine added, "I know Wally did not want a public funeral, because he said so forcefully and directly when we discussed specifying that in his will. We talked about every detail, including how he would be dressed this evening at Gray House."

Wally's wonderful eighteenth-century three-story frame home was called Gray House because an early Philadelphia family named Gray had built it and because it was painted gray.

"I can confirm the character trait but not the no-funeral request," R said. "I had no discussions with Wally about that."

Clymer said to Paine, "Wally was a man of flourish, ceremony, and precedent. I don't get it."

But R did. "It has to do with the size of the crowd, doesn't it, Bill?" he said.

"I'm afraid so," Paine said, clearly grateful that he was not going to have to say the embarrassing words himself.

"More than twenty thousand people came to Ben's very public funeral two hundred and thirteen years ago," R said, "and unless Wally's could reach something like the same number, forget it. Is that it?"

Bill Paine nodded. That was it.

"Then the answer, quite obviously, is to make damned

least twenty thousand mourners attend," said Elbridge Clymer. He was buoyant, lit, ready for the challenge. Little shots of heat seemed to be rising up from between the short spikes of his dark-brown hair, reminding R of a *New York Times* line in its story on Clymer's BFU appointment. "As a white male, the only diversity history his hiring makes is that he will be the first president of an elite East Coast university to wear his hair in a crew cut."

R figured that, to match Ben's funeral turnout, Clymer would have to promise straight As to the entire BFU student body in exchange for attending, as well as coerce City Hall into ordering every city employee—including police and firemen—to be there.

Wallace Stephen Rush, Ph.D., was not a Philadelphia Philly, Eagle, or 76er. He wasn't a native hero, like Sylvester "Rocky" Stallone or even Bruce Springsteen from neighboring New Jersey. He was a historian, a professor, a teller of stories, a wit who had devoted his life to Benjamin Franklin. He was responsible for five books about the man some hailed as the First American, including *Ben One* and *Ben Two,* which taken together were considered by most experts to be the definitive work. "There's probably nothing more to know about Benjamin Franklin," said the *Washington Post* reviewer of the Pulitzer-winning *Ben Two. Ben One* had been a Pulitzer finalist five years earlier.

> Dr. Rush appears to have run down every scrap of information there is about Franklin. It seems likely there are no more sources, no new places for future researchers to go, no angles or perspectives, no revelations of information or opinion to bring to the man, the accomplishments, the legacy of Benjamin Franklin.

R enjoyed those words at the time, but he knew better. The search for what is new and revelatory is the grist of all history. There is never an end. Look at the recent new material from

Bernard Bailyn, Gordon Wood, and Joseph Ellis on that whole revolutionary period. And what about Ellis's previous book on Jefferson, David McCullough's enormously successful work on Adams, Paul Nagel's before that on John Quincy Adams, and even the most recent books on Franklin by Wood, Claude-Anne Lopez, H. W. Brands, James Srodes, Edmund S. Morgan, and Walter Isaacson? The curiosity and new information about the events and people of our national beginnings will never cease.

There had indeed been considerable publicity about Wally through the years, and he had hosted several Franklin specials and discussion programs on WHYY, the local public television station. His most important national exposure was as one of a dozen on-camera experts interviewed on a recent four-hour PBS miniseries on Ben. But he was not the kind of celebrity whose demise would draw 20,000 people. Most likely, thought R, not even a service for Stallone or Springsteen would do that. Three hundred or so for sure and possibly as many as a thousand, but that was it for Wally, who clearly knew this also; thus his desire to skip a public event that would appear puny compared to Ben's.

"What do you think, R?" It was Bill Paine. "Do we ignore Wally and let Elbow try to top twenty thousand?" *Elbow* was Elbridge Clymer's nickname, one that had been with him since high school. The origins, he had told R, were an understandable wish not to be called Elbridge and his aggressive use of elbows when he played basketball. The subject of nicknames had come up a few months previous at a BFU alumni dinner in Washington. Clymer asked R why he went by an initial, to which R responded with his now tired line about hating his first name, Reginald, more than even Raymond, his second.

R had never been good at meetings. A low regard for them was one of the reasons he enjoyed his mostly solitary work as historian and writer. He found meetings among his own kind to be mostly a means for exchanging hostilities and inanities under cover of an atmosphere that encouraged witticism over wisdom, show over substance. And yet, counting the Rebecca adventure, here he was attending the second of two high-octane meetings in one day.

"What do you think, Harry?" R said, throwing the funeral-size ball over to Harry Dickinson, Wally's longtime book editor. Harry, nearly seventy in age but under thirty in energy and vigor, had come down from New York this morning. Harry was known by his friends as the Bush because most everything about him was bushy: his graying brown hair, his eyebrows, his checked sport jackets and flannel slacks. He also seemed to shuffle sideways, rather than walking straight ahead, as a bush probably would—if it could.

"I think Wally wouldn't mind as long as the twenty-thousand number was reached," said Harry.

"Fine," said R, "but it can't be done."

"We can do it!" Clymer said.

R looked around at the others. There was no *we* here, only silence from Clara Hopkins, Wally's current top assistant representing Wally's staff and looking even better than he had remembered. Not a word from two of Wally's most ancient colleagues in the BFU history department or an equally ancient cousin of Wally's childless and long-dead sister. Only polite grins from Caesar McKean, a long-time drinking buddy of Wally's who owned Philadelphia's classiest and most famous Italian restaurant, and Joyce Carter, a retired Broadway and film actress who was long rumored to be Wally's girlfriend. R knew, however, that there was nothing between them but great affection and fun. Wally's wife, Gertrude, had died twenty-five years ago in an auto accident on the Benjamin Franklin Bridge, the main artery across the Delaware River from Philadelphia to New Jersey. Wally took her death as some kind of signal or omen because it happened on the bridge named for Franklin and because Ben's wife, Deborah, had preceded him in death by many years too.

R's attention remained on Clara Hopkins, seemingly much

leggier than the last time R had seen her. Her hair was bright blond and her skirt was way too short. Her legs, exposed on the other side of the low coffee table, seemed longer than ever. Maybe her legs hadn't grown any and it was only that R was seeing more of them than he had before. Had she always been this beautiful?

"I *can* do it and I *will* do it," said Clymer, who was taking quick glances at what was visible of Clara Hopkins below the table as well.

So. Despite his wishes, there would be a very public service for Wallace Stephen Rush that would be attended, it was hoped, by at least twenty thousand people.

A major agenda item of the meeting having been resolved, Clymer leaped to his feet as if he needed to spring into action now, immediately, from this room.

"I leave it to the rest of you to begin preliminary planning for the service, which I am sure will go down in Philadelphia history as the most striking, monumental, and unforgettable memorial since the one for Ben himself," said Clymer. "My immediate mission is to assemble the mourning crowd."

He said he would see everyone this evening at Gray House and gave cursory farewells to the others. But he gestured for R to come with him. It was the time-recognized—and annoying—signal for saying, I need to talk to *you* about something too important and too sensitive for the ears of these lesser beings.

. . .

There was another person with a private message for R. Bill Paine took R by the arm and guided him away from the flow with Clymer and gently halted him against a hallway wall.

"Wally has made you his literary executor, R," Paine whispered.

That was not a surprise. Wally had talked to R about it, and R had even discussed the probability with Samantha, his historian fiancée—of sorts—who was away at the moment on her own writing project about John Hancock.

"I'm honored," R whispered back.

"Another thing Wally did does more than just honor you," Paine added. "He upped your share of the royalties on *Ben Two* from the current fifty percent to a full hundred percent. As you know, there are already more than three million copies in print, in twenty-three languages, and more to come."

"That was very generous of Wally," R said, trying his best to hide his surprise at the news. This was something he had definitely *not* discussed with Wally.

Then Paine reached inside a breast pocket of his suit coat, extracted a white envelope, and handed it to R. "Wally asked that I give this to you upon his death."

R took the letter and put it in his own coat pocket without looking at it, except to notice the seal. There was a dab of red wax, the size of a quarter, over the pointed part of the envelope flap. Wally was either playing historian games or wanted to make damn sure nobody else read what was inside.

"Brace yourself for seeing Wally tonight, R." Bill Paine gave a wave and departed before R could comment. Why should he brace himself? He'd seen dead people before.

. . .

Moments later, R was behind a closed door with Elbow Clymer.

Still radiating heat and excitement, Clymer said, "I hereby officially offer you a tenured position at your alma mater, Benjamin Franklin University. This involves a newly created chair and an institute dedicated solely to research on Franklin and named for Wally. The recent new public interest in Ben—*Time* and *Newsweek* magazine covers and all the rest—that will climax with a crescendo in 2006 with the three-hundredth anniversary of his birth, make it a perfect time to establish this institute. Everything you want goes with it. I will personally raise the money to fund whatever research and whatever staff and resources you desire. Write your own ticket, and I will take it at the door and punch it, like a dutiful train conductor."

A little earlier today on the Metroliner from Washington—now an analogical coincidence of the first order—it had occurred to R that Clymer might make such a pitch. R's long relationship with Wally, the university, the American Revolution, and Franklin scholarship made it a natural. But he had put such thoughts aside for the ninety-minute train ride to concentrate on what he was going to do about Samantha. She was away working on her John Hancock book, but when she returned he was going to have to come to grips with his pre-separation belief that God may not have intended them to be man and wife after all.

"You not only have the university's permission but also its encouragement to appear as a commentator on television," said Clymer. "If it will make it easier, we will construct a television studio and satellite uplink for you and your colleagues right in your offices. CNN, Fox, MSNBC, and the world will be at your fingertips."

"I don't do much TV," R said.

"You will now," Clymer responded.

R was ready to quote John Gwinnett on historians speaking on television much too often about things they knew much too little about. But this wasn't what really mattered.

"The main thing is, I don't do tenured professorships," said R. "I don't like the structure, the politics, the malice, the games, the chains, the meetings—"

"But don't forget the unforgettable: the need for a healthy steady income," said Clymer. "I can assure you that the compensation package we organize will make you very happy."

R smiled. It was the polite—and expected—thing to do. He could not say to Elbow that the news he had just received from Bill Paine about the *Ben Two* royalties might make it unnecessary for him ever again to do something just for the money.

Elbow Clymer raised his right hand. "Just agree to think about it, R. That's all I ask for now." He lowered his hand as if signaling a subject change. "That young woman in there who worked for Wally—what's her name?"

"Clara Hopkins."

"That's a pretty name: old-fashioned, steady. My ex-wife's name is Myrtle. We divorced last year."

Clymer disappeared and R rejoined the others in the library—to work out the details of what would happen at the striking, monumental, and unforgettable funeral for Wallace Stephen Rush and to admire the legs of the young woman with the pretty name.

. . .

R waited until he was back in his room at the nearby Chestnut Hotel before breaking the wax seal and removing Wally's letter from its envelope.

His was immediately overcome with a feeling of profound sadness. There were three folded pages of lined schoolboy notebook paper, and Wally had clearly tried with much difficulty to keep his writing between the lines. R could feel the hurt, the extreme agony it must have put the old man through for him to do this. Wally's handwriting, once precise, firm, and almost as clear as his typing, was on these pages faint in places, loopy, erratic, and shaky, similar to that found in a sloppy first-grader's penmanship workbook.

There was no date at the top of the first page. Because the writing got progressively worse with each few paragraphs, it was obviously not written in one sitting. R couldn't even imagine how many hours and days of painful writing it must have taken Wally to do it.

R read:

My dear friend:

Forgive the way this looks. I'm embarrassed that I can barely hold a pen in my hand and make it move the way I want. But I had no choice but to do it this way because it could not go through a computer, a tape recorder, or, even more important, a secretary or any other person. Only your eyes, mind, and sensibilities can be exposed to what I have to say.

But before I get to the hard part, I'll bet anything you and my other friends are not doing what I wanted about sending me off to the heavens—or wherever. I'm right, aren't I? People always think they know what is best for the corpse better than the deceased himself. Tell everyone I will come back as Aaron Burr and fire a big fat hole into anyone who screws with my wishes. The big issue for me is the cremation and private service. I want no report in the Inquirer *that Wally Rush had a huge public funeral and nobody came. Forget Burr. Use Adams instead. Tell them I'll return as John Adams and lecture them to death.*

But that is not the purpose of this letter.

As you know, I have left instructions that you be appointed my literary executor. Decline and I'll not only do Adams and Burr, I'll add the deadly weapon of Jefferson in coming after you. Your epitaph would read: "Here lies R. Raymond Taylor, smitten dead by a ghost armed with the self-righteous imperiousness of Thomas Jefferson!"

Yes, it is important for me that you be my executor because I'm not keen on others messing around in my papers for reasons that are certainly well-known and understood by you. But there is much more to it than that.

R, I need you, Ben needs you, and history needs you to do the most important work any historian of the

American Revolution could be asked to do, now or at almost any other time. I am not exaggerating.

Something was dropped in my lap several months ago. It was very hot, too hot to tell another soul about. Certainly not anyone on my current staff or in our larger scholarly world. I decided against telling even you until now. As Ben said in one of his Poor Richard maxims: "Three may keep a secret if two of 'em are dead." In this case, there will be two keeping this secret—and one of 'em, me, is dead.

My secret, now yours and yours alone, concerns twelve handwritten pages that turned up last year. They were found sewn in the lining of an exquisite man's cloak that had been contributed to the Eastern Pennsylvania Museum of Colonial History, a very small institution in Eastville. The cloak was among the perfectly preserved personal effects of a Pennsylvania gentleman of the Revolution and had been recently contributed to the museum by the man's descendants. There is no question that the cloak is an authentic garment of revolutionary American vintage.

In the process of examining the coat for exact dating, the museum people felt, found, and extracted twelve pieces of paper from within the cloak's lining. The paper and the writing appeared to be eighteenth-century, but the words, while in English, made no obvious sense. The sentences were fragmentary; the phrases were disjointed. The only thing they could determine for certain was that Ben was the principal subject of the writings because his name—or obvious references to him—dominated the script. There were also mentions of Washington and Adams, among other founding stalwarts, but because Ben was the main

*subject the Eastville people asked me for help. Would I try
to make heads or tails of this? they asked. I, of course,
agreed and spent several hours in Eastville going over the
writings. When I finished, I declared the scribblings to
contain nothing of importance. I said they seemed to be
the diary of someone who was unidentifiable and thus of
no historical value. The museum people thanked me,
made plans to put the cloak on display, and locked up the
papers in a safe, where, as far as I know, they remain out
of sight and unstudied further.*

What I said to the Eastville museum people was a lie.

*Those papers, if I deciphered them correctly in my
hurried and difficult state, point to the possibility of
treachery and savagery by Ben of a magnitude quite
beyond what anyone, even the strongest Franklin haters
among the Adams and Jefferson crowds, could have
imagined. They appear to be the account of a meeting to
consider serious charges against Ben. The accusation,
bluntly put, is that he had a woman murdered: the mother
of William, the subject of one of your previous professional
obsessions. The best I could tell from the notes is that Ben
disposed of the woman because she was threatening to go
public with her claim of motherhood in a way that would
damage Ben's hard-won reputation as a hero of the
Revolution, Knowledge, and Mankind.*

*My lie was motivated by a knee-jerk instinct to protect
this reputation. As you know, it has taken years for
historians, both serious and popular, to give Ben his due.
He is finally coming into his own as an equal to
Washington and Jefferson; he is no longer that fat lecher
in granny glasses who made up cute little sayings, played
with kites in thunderstorms, and lusted after everything*

in a skirt. All of us Ben folks have been excited about the additional attention to his real accomplishments that should come in 2006, as his 300th birthday is celebrated. Now here was this awful development. Charges about his having been accused of murdering the mother of his illegitimate son would not only rain on his tercentennial parade, they would damage his place in history irreparably. I didn't want that to happen. So I lied.

Then, several weeks ago, the prospect of dying focused my mind—and my professional conscience. I could not go without telling somebody what I had done and ask him to study those papers and the story they tell. History demands it, whatever the truth might do to Ben's place in history.

That, R, must be your only real labor as my literary executor. I have made an adjustment in my will that should help make it possible for you to clear your calendar and make it work for you financially.

I would caution you on the obvious. I might very well have misread those papers. My mind, once among the brightest stars, is now the dimmest of nightlights. Also, the whole thing might be a setup or a hoax perpetrated by the anti-Ben crowd. They tried to turn him into a British spy, don't forget. And there was also the Prophecy. If it had not been for our efforts, there is a good chance that the false and idiotic charge that Ben made an anti-Semitic speech at the Constitutional Convention might have taken on new, maybe permanent, life.

I beg your forgiveness for putting you in such a position. But, as I said, I grew to know I had no choice. The papers must be studied, and you are the only one on the face of this earth who can do it the right way, in a fair, discreet, and credible manner.

*I urge you to go about your work in complete secrecy.
You don't have to tell Wes Braxton, for instance, why you
want to see those papers in his safe. He's the kid in charge
of the museum at present. Just tell him I mentioned them
to you and there was an outside chance they might relate
to your research—something like that. It would be a
shame if information about your investigation became
public and it then turned out to be baseless. Ben and his
tricentennial would be hurt for nothing.*

    *Thank you for doing this, R. I fervently hope that my
initial readings and impressions of what is written in the
papers are wrong and that Ben continues to soar.*

    Good luck. And God's speed.

    Yours for Ben,

    Wally

Wally. The name was written in the manner of Ben's signature, complete with his ornamental lines below.

Yours for Ben.

    *Always, Wally; always for Ben. Certainly, I will do what you
want about the Eastville papers. Haven't I always done what you
wanted? It shall be done . . .*

    Wally. Ben. Wally and Ben. Ben and Wally.

    Wally had always insisted that everyone, including students,
call him Wally the way he and most other Franklin scholar/
worshippers referred to their man simply as Ben. Wally loved contrasting that with the Jefferson acolytes, who spoke reverently in

hushed voices of *their* hero as "Mr. Jefferson"—as if he were God. Wally took pleasure in saying the distinction also fit the contrasting personalities of Common Man Franklin and Imperial Man Jefferson. "Could you ever imagine books about Jefferson with the titles, *Tom One* and *Tom Two*?" he would ask.

THREE

R arrived early at Gray House, hoping to spend some private time with Wally before anyone other than morticians and caterers were around. But whoever came in person, R knew there would be no escaping the varied presences of Ben as well as Wally.

A *Philadelphia Inquirer* feature story once described Wally's personal collection of Benjamin Franklin memorabilia as giving Gray House "the appearance of a museum—almost." From R's perspective, the look was a mix of theme junkyard and cheap curio shop—almost.

But as he mounted the front steps, R figured Wally had the right, even in his deteriorated state of mind, to do what he pleased. Why shouldn't Ben's leading biographer and worshipper be surrounded in death by likenesses of Ben himself?

True, the images were many and varied: on painted plaster death masks; on a multitude of plastic, brass, bronze, chrome, lead, glass, and wood busts of all sizes; and on a variety of cloth, leather, bobble-head, traditional, Smurf, and commemorative costumed dolls as well as salt-and-pepper shakers, lamps, lanterns, typewriter ribbon tins, cream and sugar sets, coffeepots, beer mugs, chess sets, teakettles, wind-up toys, medals, firefighting equipment, pennants, flags, money clips, stoves, bookends, Avon bottles, lightning rods, door knockers, walking-stick knobs, wax seals, oilcans, nutcrackers, tip trays, cuff links, whiskey flasks, syrup cans and bottles, switch-plate covers, pewter and bronze statuettes, flashlight batteries, kites, computer mouse pads, cell-phone covers, paperweights, wooden whirligigs, toy printing presses, piggy banks, Christmas tree ornaments, watch and clock faces, armonica sheet music, cast-iron doorstops, telescopes, chemistry sets, binoculars, and publicity photos of Pat Hingle, Robert Preston, Lloyd Bridges, George Grizzard, Richard Widmark, Melvyn Douglas, Howard da Silva, Richard Easton, David Huddleston, Dylan Baker, and other actors portraying Ben onstage, or in movies, television, and radio.

These things were all over the house but particularly on shelves and tables and windowsills in the main parlor, where the funeral director's people had laid Wally out for viewing.

There, in the center of the room amid curios, white silk, and red roses, in a polished mahogany casket, was the embalmed body of the man who had been the single most important person in R's professional life—his mentor extraordinaire. Here lay the now-spent force that had opened R's mind forever to the wonders of the Revolution, the Founding Founders, and Benjamin Franklin.

Here lay a man whose corpse could pass for Franklin's.

Wally's paunchy body was dressed in a long collarless chocolate-brown coat with matching breeches. White stockings were on his legs below the knee; white lace showed from a shirt at the top and at the cuffs. There was a modern-day necktie arranged loosely around the neck, but everything else was pure Ben. Wally's long brown hair was even combed straight back off his pudgy face and forehead and arranged on his shoulders just behind his ears. His square wire-rim glasses were in perfect place. He really was the spitting image of Benjamin Franklin.

"You did it, Wally," R said out loud. He stood alongside the casket, which was raised waist-high on a bier decorated with greenery and small flowers. "I don't know whether to laugh or cry."

R remembered when Wally changed his signature slightly to resemble Ben's flourishes and began to walk like Ben, even using a cane although he didn't need one. He switched from wearing heavy black horn-rimmed bifocals to a pair in Ben's distinctive style and commenced to overeat so he would have a Franklinesque paunch. Then he let his gray hair grow and dyed it brown, in a near match with some contemporary descriptions of Ben's hair. Once a full-throated and precise speaker, Wally even moved to a quiet flat-speaking manner—again patterned after well-documented descriptions of his hero.

Bill Paine had had no need to tell R to brace himself for what he was going to see. R was not surprised by Wally's final morphed appearance in the coffin. It was clearly the final touch, along with the April 17 death date and eighty-four-year-old death age. Ben and Wally. Ben/Wally.

"Well, whatever, there you are, Wally, you blessed man," R said. He leaned down into Wally's face, which had been fixed in a slight smile and made up with rouge and powder to appear robust. "You could pass as Ben in any *Law and Order* lineup—in appearance as well as in spirit and intellect. I honor you, my friend. I cherish you. I will miss you. And I will go to Eastville."

R's father, a Presbyterian minister in a small Connecticut town, had spoken and prayed frequently about death as something terribly sad but perfectly normal. The message: This will happen to everyone, including you, so get used to it. From the age of seven, when an uncle died, R had been expected—required, actually—to keep himself together while participating fully in the passing rites of family and friends, which included looking at their laid-out corpses. As a result, he was not ill at ease around the dead. His study of history had even raised his comfort level. How could you wonder about the lives and times of those who had gone before if you were uncomfortable with their remains?

Suddenly R's eyes fixed on Wally's necktie.

Damn! It was one of those hundred-dollar-bill ties. Some Italian entrepreneur had put them out a few years ago, despite objections from the U.S. Treasury Department, among other concerned parties. The guy had used a simple photocopy process to replicate a real $100 bill on a heavy silk material, putting Ben on the front side of the tie and Independence Hall on the back—just as on the bill itself.

This really *was* too much. R reached down to snatch the tie.

"Please, sir, let's not disturb the departed," said a man in a black suit, who appeared seemingly out of nowhere on the other side of the coffin.

"That tie is tacky and out of place," said R. But he did remove his hand from inside the casket. "I am R. Raymond Taylor, his friend and literary executor, and I have the right to remove it."

The man was young, black, and large. "I don't question your authority, sir. But I am sure that we have prepared Dr. Rush in exact accordance with his wishes. As a matter of fact, I personally worked with Dr. Rush before his death in choosing and acquiring all the clothing he wished to wear today—including the tie."

"He looks silly with that awful thing around his neck."

The young man smiled. R had to fight off a laugh himself. What could be sillier than a man dressing up like Benjamin Franklin for his viewing? Then R remembered something else— another item Wally had somewhere in his collection. It was a white T-shirt with a small portrait of Ben on the left chest and the Ben saying LOST TIME IS NEVER FOUND AGAIN lettered across the back. At least Wally didn't chose to wear *that* as part of his death costume. He also didn't swaddle himself in another possession, a huge piece of cotton fabric that was covered with colored mementos of Ben's life: a printing press, a *Poor Richard's Almanack* cover, the Treaty of Paris, Independence Hall, the Declaration of Independence, his birthplace in Boston, the Liberty Bell, a Franklin stove, a kite, a lightening rod, a horse-drawn fire wagon, and the Craven Street house in London.

R decided to be grateful for little things and move on.

"There are refreshments in the library," said the young mortuary attendant. "Go through that door up to the second floor and down the hall off the landing."

R knew where the library was. He had spent some of the best years of his life in that room with Wally and his books, his ideas, and his enthusiasms.

He had to travel a long hallway to get to the library. And on the walls everywhere were more pieces from Wally's collection. R had already been stunned by the sight of a gigantic—6-by-6-foot—plastic-coated poster that greeted everyone on entering the front hall. It was a black-and-white computer-generated portrait of Ben that resembled the one on the hundred-dollar bill. Wally supposedly bought it on the Internet from somebody in California, who claimed it had been used at a Republican Party fund-raiser at Balboa Park in San Diego. Having seen the item, R had no trouble believing the claim.

There were also other smaller framed drawings and paintings of Ben on the walls, not only in the foyer but in all the halls. Some were legitimate engravings and copies of real oil paintings; others were financial, insurance, stove, and other commercial advertisements, mostly from magazines. Some of them were accompanied by one of the thousands of Ben's sayings from *Poor Richard's Almanack* and his other writings.

The first one that caught R's eye on the way to the library was in an eight-by-ten-inch picture frame. It quoted Ben in old English script superimposed over a blue sepia reproduction of the well-known drawing of Ben flying his kite in an electrical storm: *Beer is proof that God loves us and wants us to prosper.* Next to it was a *Saturday Evening Post* ad for a washing machine that carried Ben's quote about liberty: "They that give up essential liberty to obtain a little temporary safety deserve neither liberty nor safety." R was unable to tie that to washing machines, but he had no trouble doing so to present-day Washington, D.C. R was a libertarian on matters of privacy and civil liberties and remained outraged by the words and deeds of some since the terrorist attacks of September 11, 2001. In R's opinion, these people completely misunderstood the history of freedom and individual rights in their own country.

He passed by the dining room. The last time R had been in there, Wally had a "Benjamin Franklin" 22-caliber air rifle tacked on the wall over the hutch. There had once been a full line of BB and pellet handguns manufactured by the Benjamin Franklin Firearms Company of St. Louis. But at least the room also contained a fine collection of eighteenth-century Staffordshire plates depicting either Ben or one of his sayings, as well as a full 130-piece set of Benjamin Franklin sterling silver flatware made by Towle in 1905.

Finally, the library. This was R's favorite place in the house. Yes, there was some schlock stuffed into the floor-to-ceiling shelves that covered all four walls of the 25-by-40-foot room. But there were also more than a hundred editions of Ben's famed autobiography alone, one going back to the late 1700s, considered even by Ben-haters to be one of the finest pieces of early American writing of any kind. Wally also had several original copies of *Poor Richard's Almanack* and some pamphlets that Ben had written or printed on his own press in Philadelphia. That was in addition to the many biographies and other Ben books that began with children's coloring and comic books of all vintages, plus postcards, monographs, and a full collection of the various stamps that had been issued in his honor by the U.S. Post Office through the years.

Ben had been one of the key founders of the postal service in colonial America.

"You are looking at one of the most complete private collections of printed material by and about Benjamin Franklin in the world," said a female voice from behind one side of the giant partner's desk in a far corner.

It was Clara Hopkins. R's eyes reflexively glanced downward toward her legs, but they were hidden by the desk.

Two young men in white coats and black ties were setting up a bar in the opposite corner of the room. R gave a bow in Clara's direction.

"At last count," she said, with a wink, "two thousand four hundred and fifty-six different books of varying sizes and purposes have been written about the life, accomplishments, and legacies of Benjamin Franklin of Philadelphia. They include works of fiction and nonfiction for both children and adults, scholarly and popular, political and scientific, personal and professional. There have been more books about Dr. Franklin than about any other Founding Father, including George Washington of Mount Vernon and Thomas Jefferson of Monticello. The comparative number for John Adams of Quincy, for the record, is a pitiful four hundred and fifty-eight."

R laughed. Clara had done an exact recitation of Wally's favorite opening spiel for visitors to his library.

"Did Wally cheat to make it happen yesterday?" R asked her.

"Probably, but who will ever care enough to find out?" she said.

"Pills of some kind?"

"Most likely, but I doubt that they performed a sufficiently complete autopsy on this eighty-four-year-old man with a failed liver to find out, even if he is Wally Rush."

Clara stood.

"Wally told me he was making you his literary executor. Maybe we should have a bite to eat later and go over things."

"Let's do that," said R. "Brasserie Perrier at seven?" And he turned to greet the first of the by-invitation-only guests, President Clymer of Benjamin Franklin University.

"The public ceremony is a full go," said Clymer, as he rushed to shake hands with R. Then, dropping his voice to a secretive whisper, he added, "I have some good news and some bad news on another matter. Bill Paine told me Wally left the university this house. That's the good news."

"And the bad?" R asked.

"We have to keep all his stuff in it—as is." Clymer shook his head and so did R, and then they both turned to the others now entering, two and three at a time. Bill Paine and Harry Dickinson from the planning committee were among the first arrivals. Behind them came former Wally students and assistants, prominent citizens of Philadelphia, and the Crowd: Franklin scholars from Penn, Yale, and elsewhere.

Then there was Rebecca Kendall Lee. R refused eye contact and moved quickly in the opposite direction over to Harry Dickinson.

"What are you working on right now?" Harry asked R. The editor had a vodka on the rocks in his right hand.

"A book on the early presidents—Washington, Adams, and Jefferson—and how they affect the way the presidency functions to this day," R said.

"Oh, yes, that's right," said Harry, turning away quickly and moving on.

R was more amused than offended. Harry was known as a finder, developer, and editor of prize-winning books, fiction as well as nonfiction. He was especially celebrated for his ability to help authors get early American history on the page in a way that sang—and sold. Once, in a C-Span Book Channel interview, he had even referred to himself jokingly as Harry History Channel.

But for Harry, clearly "The Opening Three Acts of the Presidency," R's working title, didn't make the grade.

R resisted a temptation to tell Harry about *Dear Audience,* a one-man Ben show he had wanted to write patterned on Hal Holbrook's *Mark Twain Tonight.* On a high school class bus trip to Hartford, R not only visited Twain's home, now a museum, he saw a special afternoon performance of Holbrook's show at the famous Bushnell Theater. The whole experience had made a lasting impression. R still had a fairly new CD and an old LP of *Mark Twain Tonight,* as well as VHS copies of two versions that were broadcast on network television. Later, as a historian, R had come to believe that dramatic performances built around important historical moments and people were very effective ways to connect young people to history.

R had dreamed of Pat Hingle playing Ben in *Dear Audience,* but the whole thing never went beyond a very rough first draft. That was because most of the Ben Crowd who read it had not been happy with it. Wally declared it "fun and possibly entertaining" but disrespectful of Ben and his legacy. To fool with it now would probably be disrespectful of Wally, too.

He saw Johnny Rutledge enter the room. Johnny had studied under Wally and then gone on to join the staff of Benjamin Franklin University Press, where he was now editor in chief and publisher. BFU had published both of R's books and several other academic ones that had been written about Ben in the last thirty years. Serious Ben books were their specialty.

R greeted Johnny with a vigorous handshake and warm manner that clearly took Johnny aback. They had been colleagues, collaborators with similar professional interests, and they were friends—but not buddies. Johnny was R's size, just under six feet tall, and in his mid-forties, but, to R, had a perpetually eager—and annoying—graduate-student look and manner. He was all corduroy, work shirt, blond hair over the ears and collar, large round rimless glasses. R, in contrast, kept his emotions as well as his dark-brown hair cropped, his clothes casually upscale and pressed. He had never had to wear glasses, not even for reading small print.

"Anything new on the search?" R asked Johnny. As a research sideline, Johnny was obsessed with running down the identity of the mother of William, Ben's illegitimate son. R had always found that quest to be interesting but not of critical importance.

Wally's letter certainly changed that.

"I'm down to trying to arrange some DNA sample work on a few possibilities," said Johnny, clearly delighted over R's interest.

"Keep me posted," said R.

"I will. You bet I will. Thanks."

"Maybe I'll give you a call someday soon," R added. And he gave Johnny a hearty we're-buddies slap on the back and moved on to speak to someone else.

His way was blocked by Rebecca. Her physical size gave the word *blocked* its full sports meaning. R, at 195, may have out-weighed her by nearly forty pounds, but the hit would have been a crunching one.

"I deserve some help, some slack from you, R," she said, her voice quiet but firm. "For simple reasons of loyalty among Wally's students and assistants, if nothing else."

R shook his head.

"What does that mean?" she asked. Some red was appearing in her cheeks.

"It means I can't talk about this with you. It's improper."

Calling on his old skills as a high school quarterback, he feinted to the left and then moved to the right.

She said as he passed by, "I swear on Wally's costumed re-mains, R, that I will not go quietly. I really meant what I said about the throwing of stones."

He just kept walking.

FOUR

Spontaneity with and toward women did not work for R. Think ahead, plan ahead, stay ahead—keep a head. Those were his guiding principles now, after a lifetime of going for the moment, the thrill. That practice had, from time to time, caused pain, put him in jeopardy, helped end his first two marriages, and was now among the things putting strain on a potential third.

I will not make a move on this woman.

That was his vow as, back in his Philadelphia hotel room, R prepared to meet Clara Hopkins for dinner at Brasserie Perrier on Walnut Street.

He had made the mistake of calling Samantha at Glenhaven, the upscale country inn in northwestern Pennsylvania. She was holed up there for three weeks to finish the first draft of her book on John Hancock. She and R shared a love of revolutionary history as well as of good chardonnay, superior scholarship, Mercedes-Benzes, Amtrak, American Express Platinum perks, and privacy. But after two and a half years of cohabitation storm and conflict over all the things they did *not* share, the relationship was falling apart.

"I'm in the middle of writing up Hancock's funeral at the moment," Samantha had announced, making it clear to R that he was interrupting. She had specifically gone to Glenhaven, the 1,200-acre estate of a wealthy oil family now open to the public, in order to avoid interruption. Unlike R, who could write anywhere anytime under almost any circumstances, Samantha required stretches of solid isolation to get the best of her writing done.

"I'm part of the group working on Wally's funeral," said R, determined to force a conversation. "Isn't that a coincidence? Here we are, both of us doing funerals at the same moment. Are you coming to Philadelphia for Wally's? It'll be on Monday—four days after his death—on the twenty-first, of course, like Ben's."

"Of course," said Samantha. "How did your inquisition of Rebecca go?"

"She was her usual Rebecca self. So was Sonya. Both of them will probably be on hand for Wally's funeral."

He pressed Samantha for an answer about *her* coming.

"Oh, I don't know," she said. "Let me see how things are going with my friend John Hancock. I don't want to lose my concentration again. Wally sure won't miss me. As you well know, he shared your disdain for Hancock and the rest of the Massachusetts group."

Yes, R knew all about Wally's strong views about the anti-Franklin leanings and whinings of John Adams and Hancock, among others. Both Hancock and Adams were persona non grata among the Ben crowd for their supposedly joking remarks about Ben's being asleep during many of the most important sessions of the Continental Congress, the Constitutional Convention, and other key events of the Revolution. It wasn't true and it wasn't funny.

"*I* will miss you—I miss you now," said R to Samantha.

Samantha only breathed into the phone. But R could read her breathing. *Liar!* it exclaimed. Samantha didn't believe for a second that he actually missed her. Nobody—no woman, that is—ever believed him when he said things like that. He saw it as the cross of his past misdeeds with women that he had to bear. Unfairly bear, for the most part, in his opinion.

"How *is* the writing coming?" said R.

"Slowly, as always," Samantha said, her voice now transmitting a fervent desire to hang up. She hated it when he asked her how the writing was coming.

"Hancock was a fascinating figure—"

"Stop it, R. We've been through this many horrible times. 'John Hancock deserves but a brief couplet or two in any history of the American Revolution,' unquote. So sayeth the great, the one, the only R. Raymond Taylor, speaking not only for himself but also for the great—and now late—one and only Wallace Stephen Rush."

Now it was R's turn just to breathe into the telephone receiver. She had quoted him accurately. That was what he believed about Hancock and, unfortunately, he hadn't been able to resist what he considered a professional obligation to tell Samantha so. It was one of those disagreements that continued to rupture their relationship. So be it. Not even love should be able to bend the integrity of a truly serious scholar of history! Yeah, yeah, yeah.

"Who have you picked up tonight?" Samantha asked.

"Samantha, please!"

"Just an early dinner in the room, a little *Law & Order* on television, and right to bed. Is that it, dearest?" Samantha's words were drenched in hostility.

"Sure, something like that. I've got my new laptop, so I might also do some work on my *Washington Post* op-ed piece. I told you about that, didn't I? They want something on why Franklin is finally getting the popular as well as the serious scholarly attention paid to Washington and Jefferson."

"You told me about thirty times—but who's counting?"

R took a deep breath of honesty and said, "I am, in fact, meeting a colleague for dinner at Brasserie Perrier."

"A female colleague?"

"Yes, Wally's chief assistant, Clara Hopkins. You probably will have met her at some function or other. She's involved in planning the post-funeral arrangements. As you know, Wally appointed me to be his literary executor. I'm pretty sure I'm going to do it. What choice do I have, really—"

R stopped talking when he realized there was no longer anyone on the other end of the line.

So much for honesty.

I will not make a move on Clara Hopkins!

A short while later they were at the restaurant. R loved the feel of Brasserie Perrier as much its food. It had a fun happy-hour bar with purple walls, velvet bar stools, and a cracked glass mirror. The dining room served high-class French food amid small columns, sparkling wall lanterns, and a huge ripoff of the painting *Nude Descending a Staircase* by Marcel Duchamp.

No matter what!

"I guess you're not going to tell me what was in the letter Bill Paine gave you?" Clara said, after they were in the dining room and into their first course and second glass of chardonnay, a dry tight 1997 Meursault.

Even if she comes on to me.

"That's right," he said lightly. "Wally wanted it kept confidential, and I believe strongly in honoring the wishes of the dead."

"That's quite an honor, being his literary executor."

Even if she propositions me.

"That's what he wanted," said R, trying to avoid touching her left knee with his right. She had moved it up to his under the table. "I haven't decided for sure whether I will accept it. I have so much on my plate right now."

How old is she anyhow? Not even thirty?

"You do so much, you really do. Books and articles and op-eds, lectures and speeches here and there. I don't know how you do it."

"I feel an obligation to Wally, though," R said.

If she's only twenty-five I'm almost fifteen years older than she is.

"Wally was worried deeply about something he had been working on concerning Ben," Clara said. "I'd bet almost anything his letter to you concerns that."

Even if she cries and pleads with me.

"No comment," said R.

"You have just confirmed it."

"I have confirmed nothing."

"I'd give anything to know what Wally was worried about. He struggled so hard to write that letter. I offered to let him dictate it to me, but no. He carried it around with him even when he slept, as if it were the secret to the atomic bomb. It must have been really important."

"Forget it, Clara," said R. "I have nothing to say about that letter."

"I *know* Wally's concern seemed to begin after he went over to a museum in Eastville to look at some papers. But he said there was nothing in the papers, nothing at all. Still, that must have had something to do with it. He was already losing it mentally and, I guess, physically as well. Maybe that was what was happening and not the papers. What do you think?"

R kept his eyes and attention on his food and drink. It was crucial to give away nothing—not a hint that she was close.

"Enough about Wally and me," he said, in his best charming move-on manner. "I understand you plan to devote yourself to Deborah Franklin. That's an interesting passion."

"I know, I know," said Clara, smiling right into R's face—into, it seemed, the DNA of his skin, eyes, eyelids, nose. "The conventional wisdom is that she was a boring woman whom Ben ignored for good reason."

R grinned knowingly and nodded. That was it exactly. No historian in his or her right mind would devote more than ten minutes to finding out anything about Deborah Franklin. In comparison, John Hancock was George Washington. This young woman's decision to probe the life of Deborah Franklin flowed directly out of a growing trend among historians to find new, newer, and newest narrow angles of historical figures and events over which to obsess. That's why Samantha went for Hancock: He was available.

"I plan to work on Deborah Franklin's story, but not to give my whole being to her," said Clara, still smiling right at R. "I plan to save my passion for living persons of the present, not dead ones of the past—even if they were married to Ben."

R was struck by how beautifully blue Clara's eyes were. They reminded him of the summer sky over his parents' retirement house in the Berkshires near Great Barrington. His dad's parishioners had hired the great architect Hugh Newell Jacobsen to design for them a white and glass delicacy of a house on a mountainside that seemed to invite the sky into every room.

The waiter came to remove their first courses. R welcomed the interruption. He whipped his captivated brown eyes from her beautiful blue eyes down to the plate where once had been a thinly sliced tomato carpaccio. Clara had put down her spoon after having sipped half of her bowl of French onion soup.

"Should I assume you're going to take Wally's place on the faculty and in the world of BFU?" whispered Clara.

"Assume nothing," said R, in a voice only slightly above a whisper. "That's always the best policy, particularly for those of us involved in historical scholarship."

She made a sound slightly below the magnitude of a laugh.

"Rest assured I am available to continue my research and other duties under a new regime," she said.

"Let's rest it there."

She seemed puzzled by that response. He meant her to be.

He took another two sips of chardonnay.

"How goes the witch hunt against Rebecca Lee?" Clara asked, in a tone no different from the one she had just used in applying—with inconclusive results—for a job. "I saw you talking to her at Gray House."

"Witch hunt?"

"Everyone knows that four out of five or twenty-one out of twenty-four or one thousand and seven out of one thousand and twelve male historians have done, now do, or will do what Rebecca did," said Clara, as the waiter set down their main course before them. "And everyone knows, of course, that ninety-five percent of what Ben himself put in his almanacs was lifted from others either in words or meaning."

"You've been well briefed, Clara," said R, a growing edge in his voice. "That's exactly Rebecca's argument."

He wanted this dinner to be over.

"Haven't you yourself, the distinguished R. Raymond Taylor, done at least once what Rebecca is accused of doing?"

"No," said R, as he quickly went to work on his spiced rubbed skate wing and roasted-pepper pomme purée in an olive vermouth sauce.

He very much wanted to get away from this young woman with the long legs.

. . .

Back in his room, R immediately opened the big TV cabinet and clicked on the set with the remote control.

No *Law & Order*. Not on NBC or any of the many cable

channels that, between them, always seem to have at least one of their many teams of cops and DAs pursuing and prosecuting bad people in New York City. Watching these one-hour episodes, mostly repeats with a variety of casts, had become one of R's obsessions, the only one involving television. It was another sticking point between him and Samantha. She couldn't understand how a man with a mind and a mission would waste both by watching mindless TV cops-and-robbers shows. He argued that *Law & Order* was anything but mindless.

It was nine-fifty. Maybe he'd get lucky and a *Law & Order* episode would be on at ten.

He muted the television sound, moved over to the desk, and switched on his laptop.

With a few clicks of the mouse he was into the file that contained his notes and the beginning draft of his *Post* op-ed piece. Samantha hated the fact that he could come back like this after an evening out and do some writing. It drove her nuts; at times she was hateful. Envy is clearly the worst of sins between writers.

On the way down through the op-ed working file, he came once again to Timothy Morton's 1977 essay on Ben in *Yesterday,* the University of Chicago's long-gone historical journal.

> For years Benjamin Franklin has been the least appreciated Founding Father. He's known mostly as the kite-flying, French-leaning, dirty old man who created electricity, firemen, libraries, stoves, and aphorisms but left the heavy intellectual and political lifting of the American Revolution to Jefferson, Washington, Adams, Madison, Hamilton, and others.
>
> This factually inaccurate and grossly unfair characterization of this remarkable man must be corrected. I hereby call upon my fellow historians and scholars to step up to the public plate and do so.

They can begin by raising hell with the fools who created that ridiculous Broadway musical *1776*. Franklin was portrayed as a buffoon whose contributions to the debate over declaring independence from Great Britain were mostly one-liners.

Second, they can proclaim that it is a national disgrace for there to be no monument in Washington, D.C., honoring Benjamin Franklin. There's not even a federal office building or major national institution of any kind that bears his name. None of his homes in Philadelphia escaped the destruction of progress, so there is no shrine comparable to Washington's Mount Vernon or Jefferson's Monticello.

Franklin was a superb writer, inventor, scientist, philosopher, politician, diplomat, and printer. Much is said, for instance, about the magnificent prose of Thomas Jefferson. That's true. But let the record reflect that Franklin's autobiography, though in the self-serving mode of the genre, is a masterpiece of the literature of its time that should be read by every American schoolchild. . . .

In twelve hundred words of clear and direct prose more than twenty-five years ago, Morton had made the case for Ben's rightful place in history that was only now being recognized.

How could he improve on what Morton had written? That was a familiar and sometimes paralyzing question of self-doubt for those historians following in the wake of others who have already churned through the same seas. That was a good analogy. He scribbled it down in a notebook he had next to the computer.

Then he caught a flicker of the familiar *Law & Order* opening on the TV set and grabbed the remote to raise the volume. The deep-voiced male announcer finished proclaiming that the criminal justice system was dependent on the police, who investigate crime, and the district attorney, who prosecutes the criminals.

From his desk, R watched transfixed as a New York garbage-man found the body of an attractive blond researcher who worked for a best-selling novelist.

He remained seemingly frozen in place as it was revealed that she was murdered by a hitman hired by the novelist, a philandering married man. The motive: fear that the researcher was about to go public with the claim that she had not only researched, she had either written most of her boss's latest best-selling novel herself or stolen it from other writers.

The writer, while the jury was out deliberating his fate, killed himself by throwing himself down in front of a *New York Times* delivery truck.

"So if the press doesn't get you one way, they get you another," said District Attorney Adam Schiff—played by actor Steven Hill—to his prosecutor colleagues Jack McCoy (Sam Waterston) and Abby Carmichael (Angie Harmon), just before the final credits rolled.

. . .

Three hours later, R was awakened from a dead sleep by the taste of skate-tasting secretions in his mouth.

Soon he was wide awake. He went back to his laptop and, in less than an hour, finished his op-ed piece and then, with a push of a key on his computer, sent it off by modem directly to *The Washington Post*.

FIVE

The twelve pieces of thick yellowed paper lay on the table in front of him. Did they contain information—an indictment—that would justify looking seriously at a charge that Benjamin Franklin, one of the greatest of all Americans, was party to the murder of his son's mother?

R was sitting with Wes Braxton, acting director of the Eastern Pennsylvania Museum of Colonial History, in a tiny conference room on the second floor of the museum in Eastview. The building, located on the town square, had once been a small dry-goods store. The museum's public display rooms were on the ground floor, its offices and storage facilities up here on the second.

Wally had it right in his last letter. This was not going to be easy, R concluded, after examining and touching these dozen pages for twenty minutes.

It was a perverse thought, but the immediate scene reminded him of his Grandmother Taylor's at Christmastime. She would always put out a huge jigsaw puzzle—sometimes a yard square—on a table in her living room. R, then called Raymond by one and all, and the other grandchildren were to contribute time and energy to finding pieces and placing them in their proper places. The idea was to have the puzzle complete and ready for full viewing by Christmas Day. She bought a new puzzle for each Christmas, most of them large scenes from the American West: Grand Canyon, Pike's Peak, the Golden Gate Bridge, Indian pueblos, cowboys riding bucking broncos. As a good woman of New England, she must have seen the puzzles as a way to broaden the horizons of her grandchildren, all of whom lived in the East.

"You're sure of the age?" R asked Braxton.

"Yes, sir, we're pretty confident about the dating," said Braxton. "What do they look like to you, Dr. Taylor?"

R was uncomfortable being called doctor, as he often was, particularly when he was teaching at BFU. He hated the way some people with Ph.D.'s went around insisting that every spoken or printed reference include *Dr.* before their name. So you went to college longer than most people and wrote a dissertation about some obscure subject? It was one of the reasons he was so happy he didn't *have* to be a college professor, though he should at least give some serious consideration to Clymer's offer to return to BFU.

On the two-hour rental-car drive out from Philadelphia this morning, R had gone over and over how living in Philadelphia would go down with Samantha, assuming living anywhere with her was still in the cards. While working on the Hancock book, she had been spending as much time in Massachusetts as she had in D.C. anyhow.

"They definitely have the feel and appearance of the period, but I'm no expert on revolutionary artifacts," R replied, fighting off a tendency to be condescending when offering such answers. "My concentration is on the people, the ideas, and the events."

Braxton's cheeks seemed to turn a suitable pink. "Certainly. Yes, sir, Dr. Taylor."

Braxton was just a kid, a tall, thin, bald, nervous kid barely thirty years old. He told R he had gone directly from getting a double bachelor's degree in museum management and early American history at Boston College to Colonial Williamsburg in Virginia. He worked there first as a costumed interpreter in the historical area and then as an associate director in the education department. Eastville was his first curator's job. Then the man who'd hired him, the director, left for the Smithsonian in Washington. With only one remaining professional, the museum board had made Braxton acting director while a search committee looked for a replacement. "They said I was too inexperienced as a fund-raiser to be a serious candidate," Braxton had said. "We're pretty broke right now. If we don't find some money soon we could close."

R reached over and picked up one of the ragged-edged pieces of paper. Each was rectangular, roughly eight by nine inches, and covered with a multitude of words and symbols that had been handwritten in tiny script—in a style commonly used in colonial America. Wally was correct about their incoherent appearance. None of the writing seemed arranged in what could be called a pattern, much less a full sentence.

"Are you aware of the great Prophecy hoax that was pulled on Ben Franklin?" R asked.

Braxton said nothing, moved nothing. He must have slept through that particular lecture at Boston College, assuming there was one.

Whatever, in his old college lecture manner, R whipped through the story of the phony diary of a delegate to the 1787 Constitutional Convention that turned up suddenly in 1934. It included the text of a virulent anti-Semitic speech titled "Prophecy" that Ben supposedly had delivered during their secret deliberations. It said Jews depress morality and commercial honesty and thus should be constitutionally banned from living in the new United States of America. "I warn you, gentlemen, if you do not exclude the Jews forever, your children and your children's children will curse you in their graves," Franklin was quoted as saying. Historians of the time were slow to react, but eventually they proved beyond any doubt that there was no diary, there was no speech, and the whole story was the creation of an American Nazi Party leader.

"A few years ago, Wally Rush and I had to set the record straight again after some speaker at an Arab youth meeting quoted from Ben Franklin's so-called Prophecy," said R. "The anti-Semitic Web sites still throw it around today, as if it's true."

Braxton had given R his full attention during the storytelling, but now, at the ending, there was a puzzled look on the young man's face.

"What has that got to do with these papers, Dr. Taylor?" he asked. "Dr. Rush said there was nothing in them that meant anything. Are you suggesting he was wrong and that they charge Benjamin Franklin with something awful?"

R had made a calculated decision about Braxton. He had decided that this inexperienced kid was at least wise enough to have looked closely at these twelve pieces of paper himself and smart enough to have seen something that, no matter what Wally said, aroused some suspicion. The words *wanton killing* appeared more than once. So did the initials B.F., among others.

"Oh, no, no, no," R said, as nonchalantly as he could. "I told the story mostly as an out-loud reminder to myself to keep the Prophecy story in mind, particularly when dealing with something that suddenly turns up after hundreds of years."

Braxton nodded his head, twice. He got that, and he seemed to accept it. But he went on. "Do you see something here that Dr. Rush didn't see?"

R chose only to shrug and say, "It's too early to say anything definitive. My interests, as you know, are in the diaries *as* diaries." R's cover story for coming here this morning had been that Wally had told him of the diaries, which were of special interest to R for possible inclusion in a book of diaries from the American Revolution.

"Those references to B.F.," Braxton persisted. "I thought at first they had to be referring to Ben Franklin, but Dr. Rush didn't think so. And what about *J.A.*, maybe for John Adams? Dr. Rush pointed out that there could be millions of people with those particular initials. Did you read the McCullough book on Adams?"

R said he did.

"It's a great book by a great man about a great man, isn't it?"

R said he agreed with Braxton, at least two-thirds of it. He was not one of those so-called professional historians who resented the success of "popular" historians like David McCullough, a man R very much admired. From R's point of view, the resenters were mostly jealous academics who claimed to be writing only for scholarly reasons but would kill to have a book on the best-seller lists. R also enjoyed reading McCullough's book on Adams. The problem was Adams himself. R, along with Wally and most other Ben scholars, could not forgive or forget Adams's contempt for Franklin. Adams thought Ben was personally immoral, professionally corrupt, and diplomatically and sinfully in the pocket of the French, among many other things. R, Wally and Company dismissed Adams's attacks, as apparently Ben himself did at the time, as symptoms of Adams's own character defects, which included rabid envy, paranoia, and profound rigidity. Ben once wrote that he considered Adams to be an honest, wise man who meant well but occasionally acted "absolutely out of his Senses."

But R said none of this to Braxton, who was still talking about these twelve pieces of paper.

"Reads like somebody did somebody in, doesn't it?" he said. "A woman, maybe, was the victim?"

"Could be, yes," said R. Braxton was as smart as he had thought, and this was not a conversation he wished to have right now. "We're a long way from even having such discussions."

R stood. He was ready to get on with what he had come to do—which was take temporary professional possession of these newly discovered papers.

With Braxton's assistance, he carefully placed each sheet between larger pieces of cardboard and then slid them in a large manila envelope, which was then fitted inside a large hard-cornered briefcase.

"I will examine them in detail, have whatever tests run that are needed and have them back to you within a few weeks," R said.

Braxton, proving again that he was no fool, had agreed enthusiastically to R's suggestion but with the request that R sign a detailed receipt, which he now did.

"I would like to see the cloak before I go—if that's all right?" R asked, once the packing and signing were completed. He had barely looked at it on the way upstairs. His focus was then on seeing the papers.

Braxton took the cloak down from the display frame. R could tell at a glance that here was truly an article of beauty and substance, fully prepared to exist for another two hundred and fifty years.

It was a heavy single-breasted greatcoat, made of stiff, tightly woven navy blue worsted wool. The inside was lined with a softer red wool, the sleeves with white linen. An attached cape, large enough when turned up to almost cover the head, had red plush wool sewed on its outside. There were quarter-sized covered buttons down the front and on the sleeves.

R was struck by the cloak's majestically permanent feel and look. Only men of substance in America wore them. This particular coat was clearly designed for a husky man, one with broad shoulders and a height of nearly six feet.

"I assume there is no question on the dating of this," said R.

"None at all. The chain of possession is clear. A Pennsylvania colony man, identified unmistakably as Joshiah Ross, had it made in London in 1754. The condition is remarkably good, so he must have been a man of means and property and probably had more than one such cloak. It was passed down through his family, with a record we have upstairs in our files, until it was given to us last year just before I arrived. I can make you a copy of that record, if you like."

R said he would appreciate it. "Who found the papers in the lining?"

"I did myself," said Braxton, with a flash of pride. "At first, I thought it was simply a thick lining. But then, the more I felt around, I could tell there was a bulge; something was in there."

R ran his fingers along the lining on the side that had obviously been sliced open to retrieve the papers. "It must have been difficult to decide to cut into this."

"It was, it really was. It scares me now to think about it. I probably should have sent it to Colonial Williamsburg or the Smithsonian or someplace like that and let them do it. But I was so excited I just went ahead myself. I cut along the seam so no damage was done . . . as you can see."

Yes, R could see that. He also said a short silent prayer of thanksgiving. It was more than possible that, if the cloak had gone to experts, the Ben-as-murderer story, if in fact these papers suggested it, would have already been on the front pages and the talk shows.

Assuming, of course, that the suggestion was serious—and credible. Having spent less than an hour with the papers and their words and symbols, R was not yet prepared to assume anything or rule out anything—including the very worst.

Braxton disappeared to make copies of the papers about Joshiah Ross and the greatcoat while R continued to study and admire this remarkable piece of clothing. Whatever the validity and significance of the papers in its lining, this cloak itself was quite a find.

On the way out several minutes later, Braxton suddenly asked R, "Do you know a Clara Hopkins at BFU?"

R stopped. "Yes. Why do you ask?"

"She called this morning and asked about these same papers. She said she worked for the late Dr. Rush, and he had mentioned coming over here to examine them. She wanted to know what he had found; she could locate no record in his files of what he might have concluded."

"What did you tell her?" R was barely breathing.

"I told her he had found nothing of significance."

"Did you tell her I was coming to look at them?"

"Oh, no. It was a very short conversation."

Relieved, R let it drop.

"My condolences to you about Dr. Rush," said Braxton. "I know the two of you were very close. The funeral is Monday?"

"It's not really a funeral. A public commemoration would be the best way to describe it. He's already been cremated—I witnessed that this morning before driving out here, as a matter of fact."

. . .

Bill Paine had insisted that R be present for the reduction to ashes of Wally's body at a South Philadelphia funeral home. State law now required that there be a "valid witness" in attendance to represent the deceased's family or estate for all cremations. That followed a scandal just across the Delaware River in a Camden, New Jersey, suburb where a near-bankrupt mortician had hidden bodies in freezers and various other spots around his place while providing ashes to his customers that were actually a combination of burned leaves and dirt.

"Do you want him dressed or undressed?" asked one of the morticians; it happened to be the same young man who had been on coffin-watch duty at the viewing.

Wally was laid out on a table that had wheels like a hospital gurney. His face was grayer—clearly the makeup had begun to wear off—but he was still in his full Ben outfit, tacky tie and all.

"Dressed," said R.

The young man frowned. "Quite some time and expense was expended in securing those clothes, sir. We most often have requests that the clothing be saved as part of the remembrance mementos of the deceased—"

"Dressed," R repeated.

The young man was silent.

"Farewell again, my friend, hero, and saint," R had said to Wally.

Then he watched, his revulsion turning to fascination, as the young mortician and three colleagues lifted the Ben-dressed body of Wallace Stephen Rush up off the table and stuck it head first into the flames of a small red-hot oven.

R had expected there to be a terrible odor of burning flesh and bones. But the only smell resembled that of charcoal in an outdoor grill.

. . .

Whatever the awfulness of the details, thank God for that cremation, R thought now. He might have had difficulty facing even Wally's grotesquely costumed corpse after what he had just seen in this first cursory examination of the twelve pieces of paper from the cloak.

As he pulled out of the small parking lot behind the Eastville museum building and headed for the Philadelphia highway, he said, several times out loud, "Remember the Prophecy. Remember the Prophecy."

That helped only a little bit.

SIX

R watched from a window in the administration building as the mourners gathered on the campus green for the beginning of Wally Day, so proclaimed by Benjamin Franklin University and the City of Philadelphia. The weather was perfect, sunny with temperatures in the mid 60s, but with less than a hour left before the ten o'clock start time, there didn't seem to be more than a few hundred people outside. And most of them, it appeared to R, were BFU students, presumably enticed or coerced into showing up.

"I'd say you have roughly nineteen thousand four hundred and thirty more to go, Elbow," R said quietly to Clymer, when he joined R at the window.

"Fret not, sir," said Clymer, with an air of good humor and confidence that so far did not seem justified. "I understand they're already assembling at the burial ground at Fifth and Arch, and along Third and Fourth, and on Market to see our little procession."

R had assembled with the dozen or so other members of the official party in Clymer's large second-floor office. These were the people who would speak or otherwise participate, either in the first event here at BFU or the second one at Christ Church Burial Ground. There were coffee, tea, and juices and trays of Danish, doughnuts, and low-fat muffins for everyone. It had the feel to R of a platform party robing at a college commencement.

A major difference, of course, was the fact that only one person was the object of this attention. Wally was present in the form of a mug-sized "Benjamin Franklin" Wedgwood sugar bowl that was filled with his ashes.

They were carried downstairs and out to the platform by Clara Hopkins for the ceremony.

"In keeping with the beliefs of the man we honor here today, we will open this service with a minute of silent prayer," said Clymer, the master of ceremonies for the occasion. Neither Ben nor Wally were churchgoers or believers in much of anything religious, but since BFU had begun its life with the support of many important Quakers of Philadelphia, R and his fellow planners had deemed a Friends' moment of silence an appropriate way to begin.

A small group from the BFU band—in blue jeans and similar clothes rather than uniforms—blared out "Seventy-six Trombones" from Meredith Willson's *The Music Man*. R could not recall ever having been present when Wally listened to any kind of music. Neither could anyone else on the planning committee. Somebody suggested playing a song from *1776* but R had quickly scotched that idea. So the Willson song was chosen, mostly in the hope that its Pied Piper effect would inspire mourners at the green to join the procession. The idea of trying to add some glass-made music to the band, in honor of Ben's invention of the armonica, was scrubbed when neither suitable instruments nor players could be located.

Only the participants on the platform had seats. The mourners below had to stand. This was done for space reasons—the green was small—and also to facilitate the seven-block march afterward to Christ Church Burial Ground.

R could tell from their reactions that "Seventy-six Trombones" was not a well-known piece of music among the students. But there were several familiar BFU and professional historian faces—including that of Rebecca Lee, unfortunately, as well as those of John Gwinnett, Joe Hooper, and Sonya Lyman—out there in the crowd. He avoided eye contact with Rebecca, but he smiled and nodded at several others while the band played.

Samantha had left a message at the hotel that she was not coming today because she could not risk letting "my Hancock work get cold." It was just as well. R had to get to work immediately and intensely on those Eastville museum papers. There would be no time to play or even to make up once again with Samantha—if either party even wanted to. Goodbye, Samantha?

Clymer had given the four speakers strict instructions to be brief, to speak three minutes or less. Remember, he said, that everybody out there has to stand, and we want everyone to hang in for the procession and the second event.

Philadelphia Mayor George Rodney, the first speaker, immediately broke the rules. He talked for almost five minutes, barely mentioning Wally or Ben except to express the hope that the coming Franklin Tricentennial would bring millions of "fresh pilgrims to our mecca of U.S. and Benjamin Franklin history." Then he went off on the need for Philadelphians to come together to fix their public schools. It was the mayor's albatross and obsession.

Tom Middleton, who spoke next, came in right at three minutes. He was a president emeritus of the university and the man who had brought Wally to BFU from Yale. They were never close friends but they had had a healthy, respectful relationship that helped them survive many disagreements. The most long-lasting and enjoyable one was over whether Benjamin Franklin really deserved to be called a scientist. Middleton, a distinguished physicist, didn't think so. He saw Franklin as an extremely talented dilettante who followed his burning curiosity about electricity, the Gulf Stream, and a long list of other mysteries to discoveries that were those of a fortunate amateur. Middleton and Wally loved to debate the issue in private and, once or twice, even did so before small discreet campus groups. (Tom Middleton, as president of a university named for Benjamin Franklin, felt he had to refrain from expressing himself on the issue in public. It would be bad for fundraising, if nothing else.)

The name of the university itself was another source of friction between Wally and Middleton. When Middleton came in the early sixties, the school was known either as BFU or Franklin University. Some students, in the spirit of those times, found a way to make mischief by dropping the *B*. Alumni and parents did not appreciate the humor, and finally Middleton proclaimed that the university, in keeping with its treasured heritage and in deference to its founder and namesake, would forevermore be known as Benjamin Franklin University in all matters formal and informal, and its initials would always be BFU. Items containing "designations designed to distort the university's name for profane purposes" would be confiscated by campus security, and persons "involved with their dissemination or display" would be subject to disciplinary action. The issue triggered a small storm with some freespeech protest and debate on campus that was chronicled by mostly good-humored publicity in Philadelphia and elsewhere.

Can anybody think of a more appropriate fight to have in Ben's name? Wally asked in an *Almanack* story. The statement brought him a private rebuke from Middleton, but the storm around the profanity quickly passed with the times, and the school had been solidly Benjamin Franklin University and BFU ever since.

"When it comes time to tally the score of *my* life as we are doing for Wally Rush today, it is my hope that foremost on the scoreboard will be the fact that I brought Wally to Benjamin

Franklin University," was Middleton's major statement in his remarks at the memorial. He was a spare man but vibrant and strong, despite, by R's calculations, being over eighty years old.

Then Evelyn Ross-Floyd stepped to the microphone. She was a tall handsome woman in her sixties who was as dedicated to Ben as Wally was. She had worked for years on the Franklin papers at Yale and produced two beautifully written books about Ben, mostly from the personal angle. Wally and Evelyn had exchanged thousands of words and ideas about their man through the years. R always believed that Wally was in love with Evelyn, something Wally never denied or, as far as R knew, ever acted upon. Both were happily married to others and there was also no sign that Evelyn was interested in anything more than an exchange of Ben material and thoughts with Wally.

During her three minutes, Evelyn said, "There have been some great American pairings through the years. George and Gracie, Dean and Jerry, Tom and Jerry, Chet and David, Maris and Mantle, Ginger and Fred, Merrill and Lynch, Barnes and Noble, Rodgers and Hammerstein, franks and beans. I would submit that on the master list should also go Ben and Wally. They were two of a wonderful kind, two men with brains and humor, two geniuses of the real world—and, to be most personal, two of the most important men in my life."

R was the fourth and last speaker. He took only two and half of his three minutes, using mostly paraphrased lines from his *Washington Post* op-ed piece to proclaim the long-awaited coming of Benjamin Franklin's turn to be appreciated. He gave Wally much credit for spearheading this effort and said, "Ben lives now because Wally lived."

Then Clymer shouted to the crowd, "Onward to Christ Church Burial Ground!"

The band struck up "Seventy-six Trombones" again and, with

Clymer and the platform group walking five abreast in front of the band, the procession stepped off for the last act.

Leading the procession was Billy Heyward, Philadelphia's popular faux Ben Franklin, a local actor who made a living dressing up and playing Ben Franklin for civic, student, and tourist groups. He had also done some recordings of Ben's writings and, though he was not of Pat Hingle's caliber as an actor, R thought he was a serious person. There had been some spirited debate among the planning committee about using Billy this morning. A Quaker-like consensus finally concluded that, considering Wally's own dress-up exit, such a thing would have appealed to him. Billy might even help draw a crowd.

But it hadn't worked.

As best as R could tell from glancing behind, most of the folks on the green did fall in for the walk. But that was about it, except for people who were out on the streets anyhow and the cops who were stopping traffic at the intersections.

R's attention and thoughts went immediately beyond what was there in the present. That's what always happened to him when he walked in Philadelphia, on London's Craven Street, or anywhere else where he knew the history well. It went with being a historian, particularly one trained by Wally Rush. "You must not only be able to see and read history," went the Wally mantra, "you must also feel it, smell it, hear it, speak it."

Now, as they moved west on Market, a major downtown street, R did not really see the stoplights or the cars, the office supply stores, banks, and restaurants. Instead, he saw a narrow brick and dirt roadway teeming with horse-drawn carriages and gentry in long coats and skirts. He saw Ben making his way from his print shop, passing by the home of the Reads, most particularly Deborah Read, who became Ben's common-law wife. R considered calling out to him, "Hey, Ben, how's the day going?" At the peak of his own research and particularly at Craven Street, R often had conversations with Ben.

Now Ben turned into the courtyard halfway between Third and Fourth to the house a couple of hundred feet off Market where he, Deborah, and various members of their extended family lived. The house was destroyed in the early 1800s, but the Park Service had constructed an underground Franklin museum and other tourist structures on the site. R imagined the real thing, the way the house and the courtyard looked when Ben was there.

Then, when the procession turned up Fourth, there came into R's imagined sight pairs of wigged, arguing men on their way south toward the State House, later called Independence Hall, for debate on the Declaration of Independence.

About the time they got to Arch Street and turned back west toward the burial ground, R realized that he had not said more than a few words to his march companions, Clara Hopkins, who was carrying Wally's ashes on his left, and Evelyn Ross-Floyd on the right. If it had been a Georgetown dinner party back in Washington, he would have been in trouble for not talking to the ladies in proper alternating order.

"I loved what you said about Wally," R said to Evelyn.

"Thank you, R. You were right in saying Ben is finally getting the attention he deserves. I blame most of what happened before on Adams and Jefferson, don't you? They poisoned the well, and it's taken us this long to clean it up."

R agreed and turned to Clara.

"Don't drop it," he said, nodding toward the bowl she was holding tightly with both hands against her stomach. Clara was given the honor of carrying the ashes after Harry Dickinson had argued that it was poignantly fitting for a pretty young woman to perform that duty; Elbow Clymer had then persuaded everyone that Clara was the perfect particular young lady.

"That's not funny. I once dropped a bowl of hot bean soup at a fancy party my mother was having," Clara said to R. "I've had nightmares about it ever since."

R smiled and asked Evelyn why, above all other reasons, had Adams hated Ben so? Evelyn was known for abhorring small talk. She wanted only conversation about worthy subjects—which to her meant mostly only matters concerning Ben and the American Revolution.

"Jealousy, pure and simple. Ben was a man of the world, of the mind, and of science, as well as of politics and diplomacy. Adams was a man of Quincy, Massachusetts, who loved the law, the Revolution, and the sound of his own voice. Most everybody loved Ben, but few people other than his wife, Abigail, loved John."

Back to Clara. But before R could say anything, she said, "I won't be around tomorrow, in the unlikely event you need me."

"Why's that?"

"I'm going over to Eastville for a job interview. They've got an opening for director. I just found out about it yesterday, so I'm late to the chase. Of course, I wasn't sure I was even going to need a new job until—"

And at that moment Billy Heyward, aka Ben Franklin, motioned for the procession to stop. They had arrived at Christ Church Burial Ground.

. . .

Clara and Evelyn moved forward with Elbridge Clymer to a small two-foot-high wooden platform. It had been erected at the back side of the red brick wall around the burial ground so everyone in the expected crowd of thousands could see the ceremony.

Clymer grabbed the hand microphone from a portable public address system. Waving his arms, he asked the crowd to fan out in front of the platform. R looked around. He doubted there were even a thousand people there in the street, which the police had blocked off from traffic.

"As you know, ladies and gentlemen," Clymer said, once everyone had gathered. "We are here at the northwest corner of Christ Church Burial Ground, a remarkable two acres of history that is the last resting place for more than four thousand people from our revolutionary and colonial past."

Clymer faced to his right toward a black wrought-iron fence that spanned a ten-foot-wide break in the brick wall. "I know I don't have to tell you that one of the four signers of the Declaration of Independence buried here is the one, the only, Benjamin Franklin."

There was applause. Somebody yelled, "Let's hear it for Ben!" A cheer rose. "Ben! Ben! Ben!" And another and another.

Oh, my God, how Wally would have loved this, thought R.

Clymer, looking about as happy as R had ever seen a college president except during football team victories, waited until it was quiet again before continuing.

"Ben's grave is just inside. People have come here for years and, as many of you know, a custom has grown up of tossing a penny on his gravestone for good luck."

Again, the crowd chanted, "Ben! Ben! Ben!" and R thanked God for creating college students.

"Our cherished Wally Rush wanted something special done with his ashes. Doctors Hopkins and Ross-Floyd will now carry out Wally's wish—"

Clara Hopkins had a Ph.D.? It didn't matter but R simply hadn't known.

"—but they will do so in accordance with the request of the overseers of the burial ground that the penny tradition be followed and no new precedents be set."

Bill Paine had negotiated what happened next. Clymer moved away, and Clara and Evelyn took his place in front of the microphone.

Clara lifted up the glass bowl. "Wally's ashes are in here."

Evelyn held a penny between the thumb and forefinger of her right hand. "This is a penny."

Clara lowered the bowl; Evelyn removed the lid and dropped the penny inside.

There was absolute silence.

Clara shook the bowl, moving the contents around.

After only a few seconds, Evelyn reached down into the bowl and took out the penny, now covered with the ashes of Wally Rush. She held it briefly high over her head, turned back toward the burial ground, stepped down, and walked toward the iron bars.

Somebody hollered, "Go! Go! Go!"

The crowd picked up the chant: "Go! Go! Go!"

Evelyn reached her right hand through two of the vertical bars and, with an underhand throw, tossed the ash-laden penny onto the flat surface of the five-inch-high white stone slab that covered Ben's grave. There was an identical one next to it for his wife, Deborah.

The only words were on top of Ben's:

BENJAMIN
And   FRANKLIN
DEBORAH
1790

Wally was correct in his letter to R about a much more extensive epitaph Ben had written for himself that he chose not to use. Etched later in a wall behind the graves, it said:

The Body of
B. Franklin,
Printer,
Like the Cover of an old Book,
Its contents torn out,

And stript of its Lettering and Gilding,
Lies here, Food for Worms.
But the Work shall not be wholly lost,
For it will, as he believ'd, appear once more,
In a new & more perfect Edition,
Corrected and Amended
By the Author.
He was born on January 6, 1706
Died 17__

Evelyn was a good shot. The penny landed flat and near the center of Ben's stone.

Clymer cued the band. It played and the crowd sang:

> "For he's a Wally good fellow,
> For he's a Wally good fellow,
> For he a Wally good fe-ello . . .
> That nobody can deny."

"Let's hear it for Wally!" someone yelled. It was a kid standing right behind R, probably Wally's student.

"Wally! Wally! Wally!"

Then, "Ben! Ben! Ben!"

"Ben and Wally! Wally and Ben! Ben and Wally!"

Clymer let the cheering go on a little while and then signaled for quiet, pointed once again for music, and led everyone in the first verse of "America."

> "My country 'tis of thee,
> Sweet land of liberty,
> Of thee I sing.
> Land where my fathers died,
> Land of the Pilgrim's Pride,

From every mountainside
Let freedom ring."

Clymer signaled for quiet again and said, "Listen."

From all directions came the sound of bells ringing. How he got all the downtown Philadelphia churches to do this on some kind of cue, who knows?

R, not a man of emotion and tears, lost control and lowered his head in embarrassment. Not since childhood had he cried in public.

. . .

R was in a loose, informal cluster of people headed south toward the BFU campus and, by invitation, to have food and drink at the president's house. He was talking to no one, paying attention to no one. His thoughts were elsewhere—on Wally, on how wonderful this Wally day had been, on Clara, on the potential awfulness in the papers from the cloak, and, again, on how these streets once rocked with the noises and smells of revolution and freedom. Ben, regardless of personal sins, was here when the chips were down, and so were Washington, Jefferson, Madison, and, yes, Adams. Even Hancock. America, America! From every mountainside let freedom ring indeed . . .

"Hey, R." He felt a warm mass against the right side of his body and turned to see the large presence of Rebecca Lee striding alongside him.

"I don't want to talk now," he said.

"I just want to give you something." She pushed a sealed white business-size envelope toward him.

"Please, Rebecca, I can't accept anything about your case. It's all got to come officially through Gwinnett. Leave me the hell alone."

"What's in this isn't about me, dear R, it's about you."

Me? He took the envelope and Rebecca moved off.

He stuck the thing in an inside coat pocket and kept walking. *Me?*...

"I'm going to stop here for a moment," R said a few minutes later, to no one in particular, and stepped away from the others toward the front door of a hotel: the Independence. He figured anyone who heard or noticed him peeling off would assume he couldn't wait a few more blocks before going to the bathroom.

He already had the envelope in his hand and opened by the time he sat down in an overstuffed chair in a far corner of the lobby.

GOTCHA! was written on a small piece of white memo-pad paper clipped to two larger pieces of paper, both Xerox copies of print articles.

The first was of R's piece that had just run on the *Washington Post*'s op-ed page. Someone had used a bright red Marks-a-Lot to highlight three or four sentences.

The second was Timothy Morton's twenty-six-year-old essay about Ben in *Yesterday* magazine. It too had red highlighting through some of the sentences and phrases.

R held one in each hand and read what was under the red markings.

He had written: "After years of being the least honored of the Founding Fathers, Benjamin Franklin is finally getting the attention he deserves."

Morton had written: "For years Benjamin Franklin has been the least appreciated Founding Father."

There were three other pairings.

R: "Once he was known mostly as a woman-obsessed man who flew kites, loved the French, discovered electricity, and made up cute sayings while Washington, Jefferson, and the others did the monumental work of rebelling against the British."

Morton: "He's known mostly as the kite-flying, French-leaning dirty old man who created electricity, firemen, libraries, stoves, and aphorisms but left the heavy intellectual and political lifting of the American Revolution to Jefferson, Washington, Adams, Madison, Hamilton, and others."

R: "Benjamin Franklin was as accomplished a writer as Thomas Jefferson. He was also a scientist, an inventor, a diplomat, a printer."

Morton: "Franklin was a superb writer, inventor, scientist, philosopher, politician, diplomat, and printer. Much is said, for instance, about the magnificent prose of Thomas Jefferson. That's true. But . . ."

R: "The failure to erect a monument to Benjamin Franklin on the National Mall in Washington remains a shame."

Morton: "Second, they can proclaim that it is a national disgrace for there to be no monument in Washington, D.C., honoring Benjamin Franklin."

Me?

At the end of her citations, Rebecca had scribbled, "Here come the stones! Knock me down and you go too!"

. . .

R went directly to Rebecca in the large white tent set up behind the president's house for the reception. She agreed to go into the house with him so they could talk.

"No way is this *Gotcha,*" he said, once they were in the deserted library where the planning for Wally Day began three days ago.

He thrust the envelope with the papers at her. She did not take them.

"There's no case against me here—certainly not plagiarism," he said. "Yes, I had reread Morton's piece shortly before I wrote my own. Some of the ideas must have lingered with me. But there was no copying, no stealing. The phraseology is remotely similar but that's an accident of osmosis. There was nothing deliberate or intentional. And I gave full credit to Morton for his points and ideas about Ben."

"Tell it to the judge, Dr. Taylor." Rebecca was smiling.

"What judge? What are you talking about?"

"I may prefer official charges against you through the ARHA."

"That's ridiculous!" R wanted to kill her. Destroy her. Extinguish her. He wanted to beat the life out of her. There, right next to where they were standing, was a foot-high heavy pewter fullbody likeness of Ben. He was holding his famous kite. The perfect weapon! *Benjamin Franklin Historian Beats Fellow Historian to Death with Franklin Statue.*

R took several long breaths. Let's not lose it here now, he lectured himself. Let's not lose everything you are and you've worked for because of this woman. Let's be cool and wise, like Ben and Wally. Let's talk this thing out.

"When you say *may,* what exactly do you mean?" he asked. "I am sure you must know any charges based on these similarities will not go anywhere except into the newspapers."

"Exactly, R. Exactly. You probably would never be officially sanctioned, but there's enough there to trigger publicity that will damage you just as badly as a finding of guilt against me would—probably even more so, because your exalted position among historians gives you farther to fall."

Well, at least she's honest about that, he thought. At least she admits she's threatening me with a sham publicity assassination. I really should grab Ben and crack open her skull.

"Do you watch cop shows on television, or are they beneath you?" Rebecca asked.

R said nothing. His appreciation of *Law & Order* was none of her business.

"Well, to borrow one of their favorite lines, Let me put something on the table," Rebecca said.

She really is going to try to blackmail me!

"I say nothing to anybody at the ARHA or anywhere else about the Morton similarities. I agree that they're not much and it's most unlikely anyone else will pick up on them. I found them because I was looking for something. There is special software for catching this kind of stuff now, did you know that? At any rate, in exchange for my silence, you see to it that the Gwinnett committee treats me fairly—and softly."

R reached over and grabbed the Ben statuette. He turned it around and over a few times.

He counted to ten, eleven, twelve—and said, "In the words of Ben, in the guise of Poor Richard, 'The most exquisite Folly is made of Wisdom spun too fine.' "

"Yes or no to my offer? Going once, going twice...."

" 'Man's tongue is soft,
And bone doth lack;
Yet a stroke therewith
May break a man's back.'

"Next thing we know you'll be walking around in a Ben suit too," Rebecca said, her face brimming with confusion—and, it appeared, a sudden drop in self-confidence.

" 'It is better to take many injuries than to give one.' "

"I won't do anything or say anything until I hear from you, R, OK? Clearly you're feeling the strain of Wally's death—and possibly other things."

" 'Haste makes waste,' " R replied.

"Also, for the record, may Wally rest in peace or not, I am going to take a close look at *Ben Two*," Rebecca said, and she left R alone in the library, still holding the metal statuette of Ben.

SEVEN

R returned to the tent to say some quick farewells before leaving to proceed with what he had believed might be the storm-like onset of a serious breakdown—of his life as well as his mind.

The only good sign was that he was on the verge of huge bursts of laughter, not of tears. There he'd been, pondering the murder of a blackmailing plagiarist with a statue of Benjamin Franklin while reciting bits of wit and wisdom from Benjamin Franklin, until recently the least appreciated of the Founding Fathers.

Funny? Yes, *very* funny.

There in front of him stood Johnny Rutledge, the man of BFU Press and the obsession with William's mother.

"I may call you sooner than I thought," R said to him. "Maybe in the next day or so, if that's all right?"

Johnny Rutledge said anything R wanted was terrific with him. But he gave R a look of annoyed curiosity. What are you up to? was the message.

R found Elbow Clymer in a circle of people, all of them rejoicing in the success of Wally Day.

"You were right," said R. "Wally deserved a public sendoff. It was perfect."

Clymer thanked R for his help and support.

"Sorry about the size of the crowd, though," added R. "You didn't make the twenty thousand target—not by a long shot."

Clymer, as he had done at the first meeting, motioned for R to come with him for a private word.

"Yes, I did," Clymer whispered as they walked, smiling the same way he had this morning when R raised the subject. It was as if he had just eaten something delicious—and secret.

He guided R over to a TV set that had been set up in a corner of the tent.

"I have this cued to the proper place on the tape."

A local television reporter was standing in front of the iron bars at the Franklin grave site. People could be seen milling about behind and around him.

Said the reporter, "A Philadelphia police spokesman estimated the total crowd for this Wally Day celebration and memorial at twenty-one thousand five hundred people."

"That's total nonsense," R said to Clymer.

"The official police estimate is all that matters."

"But it's not true. There weren't more than a thousand people out there—if that many."

Clymer put a shushing finger to his lips. "Who cares?"

"Wally would."

"No, he wouldn't. Who knows that twenty thousand were really there for Ben's funeral?"

"That's part of the historical record."

"Now, now, R. You of all people should know better than to rely on something like that. Can you really rule out the possibility that some Philadelphia cop in 1790 didn't want to do a favor for his hero Ben Franklin just like one today might do for his hero Wally Rush?"

Who was it who said, *History is nothing more than the accepted lie?* thought R. Whatever, the historical *television* record for Wallace Stephen Rush will reflect forever that 21,500 people turned out on April 21, 2003, to mourn his passing.

Blocking R and Clymer's way was Harry Dickinson. "I've had an idea for a new book," he said to R. "The title: *Ben Three.* There was *Ben One* and *Ben Two* and now comes *Ben Three.*"

"Sorry, Harry, but maybe you didn't notice: The author of the first two is now a bowl of ashes."

"*You* write *Ben Three.*"

"Great idea!" Clymer said.

R tried to shake off what he'd heard. "That wouldn't work. What would it be about?"

"What was in your *Post* op-ed—which was very good, by the way—only more. It would be about the ever-changing state of regard for Ben, but also about the knowledge and research, the growing interest, and the work Wally did. Describe in detail what happened today on the college green and just now at the burial ground: the ashes, the penny, the whole bit. See it as an update, an account of the latest news from the American Revolution and the remarkable life of the amazing Benjamin Franklin, of Philadelphia and London and Paris and the world."

R said nothing.

Clymer said, "I can't think of a better way to launch the new center—"

Harry interrupted to press his case to R. "Only you could write this book, R. Wally's protégé—and, according to what Clymer here just told me, maybe even his successor, with, as he says, a new center. I might be able to get you a nice advance. Think about it, and we'll talk seriously in a few days. OK?"

R smiled and nodded. "I've got to run." And he meant that literally. He really did want to race away from Harry and this tent and these people and his own life as fast as he could.

Harry wasn't finished. "You've already written a couple of books, haven't you? Ben's life at Craven Street and something about Ben and his bastard son, William. I'll give them a quick read."

"Our own BFU Press published them," Clymer said. "I've read them both and they're terrific."

"Do you have a commitment to BFU Press?" Harry asked.

R said he had talked to them about his early presidency project, but there was no contract. Johnny Rutledge had told R he might publish such a book, but only if R could work Ben into it as a player.

"Maybe we do a two-book deal, R. You do *Ben Three* for me; I do the presidency thing for you."

Now Harry was done. He said goodbye to R and Clymer and headed off toward the bar for more vodka.

From across the tent, R saw Clara headed his way. In a sudden burst of words, R said to Clymer, "I accept your offer to create the Wally institute on Ben."

R did not hug men and did not like being hugged by them, but here he was returning a warm one from Elbow Clymer. "What a day," said Clymer. "What a day indeed!"

Clymer took something from his coat pocket and handed it to R. "Take this," he said. It was a key. R recognized it immediately as the key to the front door of Gray House.

"It's yours—the house, the possessions, everything—to use as the first offices of the Wallace Stephen Rush Center for the Study of Benjamin Franklin."

R took the key.

Clara arrived as Clymer, his show of happiness continuing to escalate, turned to greet another guest.

"I thought you only did women," said Clara dryly.

So, in addition to having long beautiful legs, she was funny? Not up to Samantha's quality but clearly in the same league. Maybe . . .

"We just closed a fantastic deal—and then some," R said, the words fluttering out of his mouth like butterflies. "We're going to build an institute dedicated to research on the life and legacy of Ben."

"That's great," said Clara, without enthusiasm.

"That means you can cancel that interview in Eastville tomorrow," said R. "I want you to be part of my team."

Her face broke out into a Clymer-like smile. The dislike and distaste she showed at Brasserie Perrier suddenly vanished. She reached out and pulled R to her. It was a warm embrace, and he returned it.

"I shoot from both sides," he said.

They agreed to meet in the morning at Wally's house to talk more.

"Speaking of Wally," R said, "where's the sugar bowl?"

"I stuck it on a table inside the house," she said, "but it's empty now."

"Empty?"

"I tossed his ashes out little by little on the walk back from the burial ground. He's out there somewhere in the Philadelphia air."

R resisted a temptation to hug her again—and longer. But as Ben wrote in one of his almanacs:

> If Passion drives,
> Let Reason hold the Reins.

·   ·   ·

R was sitting on a bench in the sculpture garden at Penn's Landing, near where William Penn came ashore in 1682 to establish what he originally called his *Greene Country Towne* and later *Philadelphia.* Now the landing area was part of a narrow concrete-covered riverbank separated from the historic part of downtown by a freeway. It was home to a ferry dock, a Vietnam War memorial, maritime museums with dry-docked old warships, a condo, and a thirty-story hotel, among other things.

Without a thought, R had simply come out of Elbow Clymer's party tent and turned east toward the river.

He was breathing hard as if he had run the full six blocks. He was also sweating and feeling the urge to throw up. Or to throw himself into the Delaware. Or to go back to 30th Street Station and board a train to someplace. To where? Certainly not Washington or New York or Boston. Maybe a small town in Maine or Kansas or Idaho, where nobody could find him. He could change his name and get a job in a service station. Or as a short-order cook. Or a printer's apprentice like Ben. Are there still real printshops? Samantha couldn't flush him if she couldn't find him. Rebecca couldn't destroy him. Neither could he help destroy her. He couldn't take Clymer's job offer and hire Clara. Or write *Ben Three.*

Or find out for sure if Ben had William's real mother killed.

He looked up and left to the Benjamin Franklin Bridge that connected Philadelphia and Pennsylvania to Camden and New Jersey. He thought of Ben and Billy—the great man and his illegitimate son, William, the royal governor of New Jersey who remained loyal to Britain during the Revolution. It was a decision that caused a ferocious breach with his father that never healed. R had become fascinated by this father-son tragedy that ended with Ben's decision to cut William off from love, money, and dignity. Ben had taken the boy directly from birth and raised him, nourished him, pushed him, protected him. Taken him from birth where? From the womb of what woman? R, like all previous historians of the Ben-Billy story, had to tread lightly through these kinds of questions, primarily because there was no solid verifiable information on William's birth. One theory put out by Ben's enemies held that the mother was a servant woman named Barbara who worked in the Franklin house. Another maintained it was

Deborah who gave birth, but because she and Ben were not yet considered married under common law, she helped raise William as her husband's illegitimate son rather than claiming him as hers.

R felt the Gray House key in his pants pocket.

Maybe he would delay the final phase of his breakdown and, before disappearing into the waters of the Delaware or the wilds of Maine, Kansas, or Idaho as a short-order cook, do a little more work as a historian—as Wally's literary executor.

. . .

Somebody had left a few lights on, so he hollered "Hello!" several times before making his way to his final destination—Wally's library. Nobody answered. The place was empty of all living things.

Here he would begin his serious work on those twelve pieces of paper. They were in the briefcase he had picked up from his hotel room on the way over.

Here now he would honor Wally's last request.

He laid the papers out on Wally's large desk as he had with Braxton at the Eastville museum. Next to each, he put a piece of blank white copy paper that he took from a stack next to the printer attached to a computer.

What he had noticed in Eastville, almost with his first glance, as Wally must have too, was that common Revolutionary War spy techniques had been used by whoever did the writing on these sheets. Ben in Paris, and also as part of his official duties in Philadelphia, was one of several Founding Fathers who used them, both as senders and recipients.

In this case, there appeared to be a variety of simple numbers-for-words cipher systems involved, plus an early form of invisible ink, known as a *stain*. Some of it had worn off, so the end result was writing of various forms between the lines and in the margins all around the paper. There was a jumble of seemingly disconnected and often incoherent words, numbers, and symbols.

R began the first important step: bringing forward everything possible to full readable form. He knew the most common of the invisible inks used back then was made by mixing cobalt chloride, glycerine, and water. To make the writing visible required only a heating of the paper.

R took the papers to Wally's kitchen for the tricky part. He knew candles were employed during the Revolution to accomplish what he was now going to do—put heat to the paper—but R wasn't about to use candles. A few false steps could result in damage or even destruction of the pages, with their contents lost forever.

He would use modern technology—after a fashion. First, a precautionary experiment. He heated the oven on Wally's stove to just 150 degrees. Then he placed a piece of the blank white computer paper on a cookie sheet and stuck it in the oven. Through the window on the oven door, he watched; after fifteen seconds he retrieved it. The paper was warm but not damaged in any way. He could only hope that the paper from the eighteenth century would react the same way.

Page one of the real thing: onto the cookie sheet, into the oven. R watched through the window. Words were appearing. He waited a full minute before removing the sheet. He set it on the kitchen counter. There were now words and numbers literally all over the piece of paper.

Page two—again, and again, and again—he repeated the process for each of the twelve sheets of paper.

After waiting until the pages were completely cooled to room temperature, he carried them carefully—one at a time—back to the top of Wally's desk. And then, with the occasional help of Wally's high-powered magnifying glass, he read each and every word, number, and mark.

He read quickly, not for detailed content but for an overview, to get a cursory feeling for authenticity and for what these papers were really all about.

His first conclusion was that everything had been written by the same person. Both the visible and the once invisible words were in the same handwriting. Although certainly no expert, he had read enough eighteenth-century letters to be pretty sure.

The second conclusion: the writer was somebody who had been active in spying during the Revolution or, at least, was a serious student of the spycraft of the time. There was the patterned separation of what appeared to be a confusing chaos of words but which, when put together, formed the intended phrase or sentence. There was also the most common numbers game. He saw *120* several times. That, as R and all Franklin scholars knew, was the code number for Ben in some of the dispatches he sent and received while in Paris during the war. Adams's *68* was also there, as were the known numbers for Washington, Hamilton, and Madison. That was in addition to the more straightforward references to them by their initials, which Braxton had picked up from his reading, as well as to their code names. Ben's was *Light.*

So—conclusion number three—these twelve pages definitely had to do with the leading Founding Fathers.

Number four: There was no reference, in numbers or initials, to Jefferson. Why not? There were two sets of numbers that appeared to be dates in 1788. Jefferson, R knew, was in France in 1788 as the first official ambassador of the United States of America. That might explain his absence from these papers.

Number five: Ben was the main focus. R counted twenty-four mentions of his code numbers, name, and initials in the twelve pages. Adams was a remote second with ten. The others had fewer than half a dozen mentions; there were only two for Washington.

Number six: A crime had been committed—or at least alleged. That crime, as Wes Braxton had said, involved a woman.

R set down the magnifying glass and got up from the desk.

He needed a break. He needed to stop.

Wally always kept a bottle of calvados, the French brandy

made from apples, in the house. With a wink to let you know he knew better, Wally claimed it was Ben's favorite drink when in Paris. Ben was not known as a consumer of any alcohol but wine. Wine merchants have long made hay with Ben's quote: "Wine makes daily living easier, less hurried, with fewer tensions and more tolerance." On the other hand, Ben often claimed his relative abstinence was a key reason for his long life.

Whatever the truth about Ben's drinking habits, R poured an inch of calvados into a brandy glass and began an aimless pace around the room. He paid no attention to any of the books or any of the Ben stuff. His eyes were not functioning, only his brain, his conscience.

Why go on? Why know any more? Why, why, why?

R took two small sips from the glass and made three complete trips around the room before returning to the desk.

The break was over. It was either go on with these twelve pages or head for the river or the train station. There was no other choice.

He started again with page one, this time for detailed content.

With the magnifying glass, his knowledge of language patterns during the American Revolution and its spy techniques, plus some logic and educated guesswork, he painstakingly began to piece together what was being said on the twelve pages, writing out his notes in longhand with a pen on white copy paper as he went.

He had paid no attention to the time since he left Elbow Clymer's party. All he knew was that it was close to two in the afternoon when he entered Wally's house.

Now, as he laid down the magnifying glass and the pen, he knew without having to look toward the window that it was dark outside.

Without stopping for more than a few seconds to take a deep breath and delay some even darker thoughts, he read back through his notes.

— *The meeting was clearly Adams's idea. He essentially
summoned the others.*
— *Ben came. So did Washington, Hamilton, and Madison.*
— *Adams said he wanted "extraordinary charges of hei-
nous criminal acts" to be considered against Ben.*
— *They met at a private location, near but apparently not
in Philadelphia.*
— *Adams functioned as a kind of prosecutor. Washington,
Hamilton, and Madison served as judge and jury.*
— *Ben, no question, was the defendant.*
— *Adams: "Evidence of an overwhelming nature" that Ben
made a deal with a man named Button Nelson to "wan-
tonly and with inexplicable malice" murder Melissa
Anne Wolcott.*
— *Wolcott, "aged 45 or thereabouts": widow of a Captain
Wolcott of the Continental Army, daughter of Arthur
[could be MacArthur, hard to tell for sure] Harrison—
Quaker, merchant, Loyalist.*
— *Adams offered a written confession. Said it was Nelson's.
Nelson was a ship loader, down on his luck. Poor. "Had
killed before." Contacted by a man about killing the Wolcott woman. Agreed to do it for fifty British pounds—ten
pounds now, forty when deed done.*
— *Nelson's confession: Took large knife, heavy rope, and
gunnysack to woman's home on Second Street. House in
ill repair and "full of filth." Found the woman abed in a
second-floor room, smelling, sweating, and moaning
from some kind of distemper. He raised knife above her
to stab her. She said, "Ben Franklin sent you, didn't he?"
Her weak voice and thin face reminded him of "starving
mangy dog." She said, "I am the mother of William, Dr.
Franklin's only living son. I had never once before made
a demand on him, and only now do I request funds for*

*sustenance and medical care. He sends in its stead a
man with a knife to take my life." Nelson plunged knife
hard and fast down into the woman's chest. She moaned
but did not scream. He pulled the knife free and repeated
the action several times, striking as many as a dozen
blows. He wrapped the corpse up in her dirty and now
bloody bedclothes and stuffed her and the knife in a sack,
which he then tied tight with his rope. He took the sack
to a boat with oars docked at the river nearby. Said
the sack was "a load no heaver than a bundle of snow-
flakes." Used rope to attached a large rock to the sack.
Rowed downriver for nearly half an hour "past all civi-
lization" and dropped sack with the dead woman into
the Delaware.*

— *The next evening, Nelson said he met "the originator of
the deed" at Seven Seas Tavern on South Street. Man
gave him the forty pounds owed. Nelson recounted what
the woman said about Ben and William Franklin. Man,
"in the dress of a gentleman of means," raged. Told Nelson he must never repeat what the woman said. Otherwise, he would join her at the bottom of the Delaware.*

— *More Nelson: Scared, he left tavern and went straight to
the home of his brother, Roger Nelson. Repeated story
of his crime and the threat against his own life. The
brother, able to write as Nelson himself was not, put into
writing Nelson's statement. That was what Adams offered into evidence.*

— *Adams: Next day Nelson was found dead hanging from a
tree on Market Street. No note. Believed a suicide.*

— *More Adams: Roger Nelson came forward to somebody
[couldn't make out name] with his brother's confession.
Claimed his brother was murdered. Written statement
turned over to an official [name also not clear] of our*

new national government. Official declared it a fraud but made it available to Adams [just in case?].

— *"My solemn oaths and duties" required him—said Adams, of course!—to pursue. Did so in complete secrecy. [Thank you so much, John.]*

— *Adams offered another written statement, this from Roger Nelson. Said other one from brother valid. Also, repeated what brother's acquaintances said. They knew Button Nelson recently acquired a knife, a sack, and some rope—and a lot of money.*

— *Adams: Discreet inquiries at "proper places of endeavor and record" showed a Melissa Anne Wolcott, "a woman once of means but no longer same," was missing. Her house had the appearance of blood in one of the main rooms. Two women acquaintances said Melissa Anne Wolcott had "born a male child out of wedlock" when a very young woman. Whereabouts of the baby unknown. Woman's father was friendly with Ben, who was a frequent visitor to the Harrison home when Melissa was an "innocent and unspoiled girl" at the time she gave birth to the male child.*

— *Adams, prosecutor, rested case by stating that he, Adams, believed the evidence, circumstantially if not directly, showed that Ben, "though a man of much achievement in his public life, had committed two of the most heinous personal crimes known to civilized society." First, he had "violated the essence of a young woman," speculating that the "act of consummation" could well have occurred when Melissa Anne Wolcott was "a mere child." Second, he had been "a principal perpetrator" of that woman's brutal murder and possibly the demise of an accomplice as well.*

— *Ben, in his defense, spoke briefly. Said he was "an old*

*and dying man who had lived a life that he was pleased
to say had resonance within large and appreciative soci-
eties of many levels both in America and in Europe."
Said he made no claim to perfection or even to attempt-
ing perfection, but he did believe he had made contributions that would have life beyond his own.*

— *More Ben: "I have nothing to say to the charges made just
now with such conviction and effectiveness" by Adams,
whom he called "a knight of freedom for whom all Americans now and forevermore will owe debts of life, liberty,
and the pursuit of happiness."*

— *Hamilton asked Adams what kind of decision or verdict
he was requesting, noting they had no legal authority to
do anything. [Amen, Alex!]*

— *Adams said he was "not wise enough to even presume he
knew what a proper course" would be.*

— *Madison asked, "Are you suggesting we be parties to
bringing formal charges against Ben with the expectation of an appropriate punishment of hanging or im-
prisonment to follow?"*

— *Adams did not respond. [Can't make it out if he did, at
least.]*

— *Solution offered. [Can't tell by whom.] By secret ballot,
each man to indicate whether to refer the case against
Ben to the proper authorities. If vote goes against such
action, each man would be bound by a most sacred word
[oath] of honor never to tell of this meeting or its subject,
even under the prospect of pain or death.*

— *Somebody [can't tell who] said, "We act together or we
remain silent forever together."*

— *The vote—three to one against action. [You were the yea,
weren't you, John?]*

— *Meeting adjourned.*

EIGHT

He heard a female voice, felt warm hands on both cheeks, and smelled perfume.

"Doctor R," said the voice, which was soothing, soft. "Good morning, dear boss of mine."

R opened his eyes to see Clara Hopkins leaning down toward him. Where was he? Oh, my God! On the couch in Wally's library.

The twelve sheets from Eastview! The notes! The summary. . . .

The briefcase. There it was, still resting on his stomach. He clutched it to him.

"What's in there, the proceeds of something terribly illicit?" Clara asked. When she got no answer she said, "All right, then, how about some coffee? Wally always had some of those instant filter things around in the kitchen. . . . I'll be right back. How do you take it?"

R sat up. "Yes, thanks, that would be great. Black—no cream, no sugar. Good morning, Clara."

He knew exactly where he was now. He remembered what happened last night. It was late—how late exactly, he had no idea—

and he had finished his writing. He had put everything in his brief-case, sat down on the couch, closed his eyes, and stretched out with the idea of resting for just a minute. . . .

"Did you spend the night on that couch?" Clara asked, as she returned with two cups of coffee.

R set the briefcase down beside him and took his cup in both hands. It was a heavy white porcelain figurine mug, made in the shape of Ben's head. He was careful to hold it so he wouldn't have to look at Ben's face, either as he drank the coffee or just held the cup. The back of Ben's head was bad enough. Did you have that woman killed, Ben? Ben! Ben! What kind of man were you?

Clara sat down in a chair off to the left.

"I hadn't intended to sleep here, really," R said, his mind hav-ing raced onward to a crucial immediate question of a much more practical nature. How much, if anything, should he tell Clara?

"What were you doing here in the first place?" she asked, try-ing her best, it seemed, to sit on what must have been a raging cu-riosity about what in the world was happening—particularly with that briefcase.

"Going over some papers," said R.

"What papers?" Clara's manner was pleasant, nonconfronta-tional. But she shifted her gaze from R's face to the briefcase. "What have you got in there?"

R made his decision: He would tell Clara nothing. Wally had chosen not to share the Eastville story with her, so neither would he. Wally certainly knew her a lot better than he did. The sole rea-son R had offered her a job was to keep her from going to Eastville, not because he really knew her or the quality of her work.

"Some personal stuff between Wally and me," he said, placing the coffee cup on a table to his left. "What time is it anyhow?" He looked at his wristwatch. "My God. It's after nine o'clock. . . . No telling how long I was asleep."

He was on his feet, the briefcase firmly held by its handle in his right hand. "Maybe we can talk later today—or tomorrow. I have a great deal to work out with Clymer about the new job. Meanwhile, I'm sure the current arrangement you had with Wally and the university will continue. No loss in health insurance, pension, parking place, football tickets, student union privileges, bookstore discounts. . . ."

He was trying to be funny. Clara was not smiling.

"Something's going on, and it's in that briefcase," she said. "If I'm going to work with you, you must feel you can trust me, you really must." This was not the come-on girl of the Brasserie Perrier. This was a woman on a serious mission.

R did not wish to lie any more than was absolutely necessary. Lies cast on calm waters tend to come back as waves. Poor Richard probably said that; if he didn't, he should have.

R said, "You're right on both counts," but he started walking toward the front hallway.

She was right behind him. "So that's it?"

"For now, yes. I have to get back to Washington."

Then he had an idea. He really did need some help if he was going to run down the validity of the Ben murder story quickly. He would do it in the need-to-know way of the CIA. He would compartmentalize.

"There *is* something you could do for me," he said, stopping at the front door.

A notebook and pen suddenly appeared from a pocket in her skirt, which—he noticed for the first time—fell well below her knees. So she didn't dress for work the same way she did for play.

"Check every colonial and city record at the Franklin Institute and everywhere else for the following names: Melissa Anne Harrison, later Wolcott; Roger Nelson; Button Nelson. All three may have lived in Philadelphia during the Revolution. If so, I want birth and death records and everything else you can come up with about them. I'm sure you know the drill."

Ignoring R's last line, Clara said, "*Button* Nelson? Button as on a blouse—or shirt?"

"That may not have been his given name, but that's all I have." He opened the door.

"I take it you're not going to tell me why you need information about these three people," Clara said.

"That's right," R replied.

.   .   .

R seldom used his cell phone on trains. During his frequent trips on the Metroliner and the new Acela up and down the East Coast, he liked to read or write—or, sometimes, simply daydream. He often went to the Quiet Cars that were on some trains, which forbade the use of cell phones or any other device—including loud mouths—that made noise.

But this morning was different. He would have an hour and half on the train to continue his pursuit of the validity of the Eastville papers. Clara's assignment was only part of what had to be done.

He had not taken the time to shave or change clothes before checking out of the hotel and hopping in a taxi to 30th Street Station. There was an 11:04 Acela to Washington. He made it with seven minutes to spare.

He found a pair of empty seats on the left side in the rear of a car. The train was not even moving yet when he went to work.

His first call was to Carter Hewes, an old graduate-school friend now at the Library of Congress who specialized in the dating of paper, ink, and other instruments of the writing and printing trade. Carter had begun his professional life as a historian for the DuPont Company in Wilmington, Delaware.

"I need to come by for a quick dating on a piece of paper," R said. "I'm on the train now from Philadelphia. I'll come right from Union Station to your place in ninety minutes or so."

"Wait a minute, wait a minute," said Carter. "How quick? I've got an alleged seventeenth-century will and testament for a guy in New York I'm looking at right now that I've been wrestling with for seven weeks, and I still haven't been able to come up with a take on whether it's real."

But Carter agreed to look at R's paper.

Call two was to Johnny Rutledge at BFU Press. R got Johnny's answering machine, so he left his cell phone and Georgetown house numbers. "It's not urgent, Johnny, but it's important. Thanks."

Then from the briefcase, R carefully removed the copies of the documents Braxton had given him that authenticated the story and chain of possession for the cloak. He had not looked at them before, because there was no need. Now there was.

Joshiah Ross. R found his name first on a copy of the original sales receipt the London tailor had issued for the cloak. The cost was ten pounds. The receipt was dated September 12, 1767. At the bottom, Ross had signed it under the words, "Taken possession this twelfth day of September, Seventeen Hundred and Sixty-seven." Ross's signature was flowing, confident, comfortable—no doubt reflecting his satisfaction with the cloak itself, R speculated. As with Philadelphia street scenes, these were the kind of speculations that came to R reflexively.

R scanned the four-page single-space typed report on which the receipt was clipped. Who was Joshiah Ross, this "man of means and position" who had that beautiful cloak made for him in London?

R raced through the text. It took only a couple of minutes for his eyes to pick out what he was looking for.

"Mr. Ross was an officer in the Continental Army, serving under George Washington. Later, toward the end of the war, he worked directly for the Committee of Secret Correspondence." That, R knew, was the name of a secret group organized to encourage and supervise the gathering of intelligence information from spies and other sources. Franklin was a member of the committee, in fact. So was Adams.

What it meant for R was that Joshiah Ross probably had the spycraft skills to produce the invisible ink and the code writing on those twelve sheets of paper.

The next find in the report: "Mr. Ross owned a farm of 3,000 acres and much produce and animal stock near Eastville. The farm remains in his family to this day." The document, R saw, was dated in 1997. Somebody at the museum or in the Ross family probably wrote it or had it written.

What *this* meant for R was that the Franklin trial, if there really was such a thing, could have occurred at Ross's farm.

Following that possibility, Ross thus—most likely without the participants' knowledge and permission—could have borne witness to the entire proceeding and then, for whatever reason, chose to produce some notes and hide them in his cloak.

For the first time since leaving Philadelphia, R looked out the window. Here came Wilmington. He had made this trip on these tracks hundreds of times, maybe thousands. But each time he saw something he had not noticed before. This time, it was a derelict bus that somebody had converted into a place to live. He didn't know one bus from another, but this one resembled an old New York City transit bus. How did it get down here? And why? Who lived in it now? Was there really no other place for this person to live in all of Wilmington, Delaware? Or could it be somebody who simply enjoyed living in old buses....

R's cell phone rang. It was Johnny Rutledge.

R got up from his seat and walked to the end of the car. There were only a dozen or so other passengers, but for his own privacy as well as theirs he decided to talk to Johnny out of everyone's hearing.

After only a brief exchange of greetings, R said to Rutledge, "Has a woman named Melissa Anne Harrison—possibly under the last name of Wolcott—showed up on your list of possible William Franklin mothers?"

"The name doesn't sound familiar—I know she definitely hasn't made the finals. She's not one of the twenty-three possibles still in the running."

"What about earlier in your research? Was she there until you eliminated her for some reason? Could you check back for me?"

There was a slightly too-long pause before Rutledge said, "You on to something I should know about, Dr. Taylor?"

"No, no. I'm just running down a loose end for a friend."

"What friend would care about stuff like this?"

"What about looking back over your earlier work, OK?"

"That'll take awhile."

"How long?"

"Well, I could do a fast name check on my computer file . . . right now, I guess, if you wanted me to."

"I want you to."

The train had made its stop in Wilmington and was now on the way to Baltimore. Leaning to get a view out a window, R saw the small stadium where the Wilmington minor league baseball team the Blue Rocks played its games. He wondered what major league team owned them—or supplied them players as a farm team. He had gone to many a game over in Pittsfield, Massachusetts, when he was growing up in Griswold, forty miles south in Connecticut. Pittsfield had a New York Mets farm team in a Class A league. Wally always said that baseball was the sport of historians. It moved slowly, and precedents, process, eccentricities, numbers, and records were as critical as winning and losing. . . .

"Here she is," said Johnny Rutledge. "Melissa Anne Harrison." R pressed the phone against his ear.

"She came up in a list I got from the old records of a colonial doctor. She was apparently from a family with some resources.

Certainly not one of the 'low girls' everybody, including Franklin himself, said he hung out with at the time."

"Give birth to a baby?"

"That's not clear. It was some kind of medical treatment."

"When?"

"On or about June 23, 1730."

William Franklin's birth date was largely accepted as being on or about then!

"So?"

"So what?"

"So why did you drop her as a possible?"

Rutledge didn't answer for a moment. "I don't remember. I'm checking."

R listened to the sound of Rutledge's computer keys in one ear and that of the speeding train in the other. The Acelas really were more quiet than the Metroliners. And the ride was softer. He looked ahead through the windows of the alcove separating his car from the next one—which was the first-class car. Up there attendants in gray uniforms were bringing food and drink to the passengers at their seats. If R wanted anything he was going to have to go in the opposite direction to the café car. No big deal, though. His business-class seat was $42 less than first class. He wasn't hungry anyhow. Who goes on a ninety-minute train ride to eat a meal?

"I see now what happened," said Rutledge. "It was a dead end."

R waited for something else.

"She was barely thirteen years old, meaning she would have had to have been impregnated when she was twelve," Rutledge went on. "No way, of course, that she would be giving birth to a baby, Ben Franklin's or anybody else's. She must have been treated by the doctor for some illness; that's why she got dropped. OK?"

"OK," said R, with a lack of force he hoped Rutledge didn't pick up on.

"You need something else?" Rutledge asked. "I'm always here for you, Dr. Taylor."

"Thank you, Dr. Rutledge."

"I saw you talking to Harry Dickinson a couple of times. You're not thinking about doing a Ben book with him, I hope."

"You have nothing to worry about, Johnny."

They said their goodbyes. R shut down his cell phone and returned to his seat as the train approached the outskirts of Baltimore—and as *he* approached a terrible possibility.

· · ·

It got worse.

First off, as R arrived at the Library of Congress, he remembered—and was struck by the awful appropriateness—of Carter Hewes's office being in the library's John Adams Building, just off Pennsylvania Avenue. Old John would have enjoyed the coincidence. Ben and Wally would not.

Then came Carter Hewes's exam of one of the twelve cloak sheets.

"It definitely has the look, texture, and feel of the eighteenth century, no question about it," he declared, in just above a whisper after only ten minutes of fingering the paper, holding it up to several shades and intensities of light, and examining it first through magnifying glasses and then with a microscope.

Carter had the voice of a monk but the appearance of a linebacker, which he had been at BFU. He was a short muscular man who wore his brown hair closely cropped and his clothes mostly unpressed. R couldn't recall ever seeing Carter in a coat and tie of any kind or combination. Carter had come to BFU to study chemistry but a couple of elective courses—one of them taught by Wally in which R was the graduate assistant—led to his burning passion for early American history. He combined his interests at DuPont, working on new ways with chemistry to conserve and preserve the artifacts of history, most particularly books and other paper materials. He had been the chief of the library's conservation division for the last four years.

Carter then qualified his declaration. "I would not swear to it unless I had the chance to give it the full treatment—put some chemicals and specific comparisons onto it so I could pinpoint its exact maker and origins."

R wasn't going to give him that chance. Maybe sometime in the future if it should become necessary, but certainly not now.

"What about the ink—the handwriting?" R pressed.

"Can't say anything conclusive about the ink either, without putting it under special lighting and doing some other little tricks of the trade, which would take awhile."

"What does it *look* like to you?"

Again, after a few more minutes dusting it with powder and staring at it, Carter said, "Seems to match the paper dating. But without knowing exactly what it's made of I can't be sure. Different inks were made of different ingredients at different times—"

R interrupted him.

"How good are you at matching handwriting?"

"Not my specialty and you know it."

"The question was, How good are you at it?"

"Pretty good, actually."

R pulled out the copy of the receipt Joshiah Ross signed for the cloak. "Did the person who signed this also write the notes on those other sheets?"

They were now sitting side by side at a large table that was tilted like a drawing board or architect's workplace. The other tests and examinations had been conducted at various other work stations in the room.

Carter put the two documents side by side. He shined a gooseneck lamp with high-beam light onto one—and then the other. Then back and forth several more times.

Then, his right hand palm up as if stopping traffic at a school crossing, he turned to R and said, "My amateur conclusion would be that, yes, both were written by the same person, or at least by a most skilled forger. But, like I said, I'm no handwriting expert. Go to the FBI for that kind of stuff."

But R was packing up his papers. He wasn't going to the FBI or anywhere else. He was going to his house in Georgetown.

•   •   •

R loved his little house, a narrow three-story red-brick Georgian that had history and location as well as comfort going for it. The place was built by a senator from Illinois in 1847, and four cabinet officers and a couple of ambassadors had lived there since. General George Marshall, the statesman of the 1940s, supposedly often dropped by for drinks with an old army friend who lived here. There was also an unconfirmed report that Kim Philby, the Soviet mole in the British foreign service, had had both sexual and espionage liaisons in the house when he was stationed in Washington.

The house was on an alley corner on a small one-way street that opened onto 31st Street and the west side of the large house where the late, great Katharine Graham once lived. R had never met her but, as a historian, he considered her autobiography one of the most honest and best of the genre. It had been his professional experience that most famous people will tell the truth about others but seldom about themselves. Mrs. Graham talked as forthrightly about herself as she did everyone else.

It wasn't until he paid off the taxi driver and was walking up the five steps to his front door that he realized what he had done. By agreeing, in a moment of a panic about Clara Hopkins's possibly going to Eastville, to taking Clymer's BFU offer, he had committed himself to moving to Philadelphia. *Living* in Philadelphia! And that would mean giving up this fabulous place.

But maybe not. As he turned the key in the front-door lock, he had a second and more pleasant revelation. It was partly with the ongoing proceeds from his half of the *Ben Two* royalties that he was able to live a life independent from the academics and, most specifically, in this nifty house. He had paid $450,000 for the place five years ago when he came to Washington to begin work on the early presidency project, and based on recent real estate sales in the neighborhood, he could probably sell it now for double that. But he might not have to do it. Those glorious checks from Harry Dickinson's Green Tree Publishers had averaged more than $175,000 a year so far. That was because both *Ben Two* and *Ben One* had become assigned reading for millions of American history students, from high school through the graduate level. Now, through Wally's will, his royalty checks might increase enough that maybe he could afford to have a really good place in Philadelphia and keep this one as well. It was a pleasant thought—a possibility. Maybe he could even figure out a way to actually live in Wally's Gray House. That would make it all the easier to keep *this* place. If, of course, he even wanted to take the BFU job. Later. He would think about all of that later.

Andrea, his Brazilian housekeeper, had come and gone for the day. The house had the luscious smell of scented cleansers and wood polish. She had stacked the day's mail on a small table in the entrance. He could look at it later. His intention now was to go upstairs, shower, shave, put on fresh clothes, and begin the serious matter of deciding what to do next about the Ben story.

Then he caught sight of a large, thick FedEx envelope on the table next to the regular mail. It was from John Gwinnett at William and Mary. The Rebecca material. The goods?

His mind jerked back to another of his real worlds, the one about Rebecca and *Me.*

Later. Yes. He would look at the Rebecca stuff later, after he had cleaned up and dressed. . . .

Forget that. He ripped open the envelope as he went to his study in the rear of the house. This was his favorite place to be in the whole world. Here were the books he had read and cherished and the photographs of the people he loved, in addition to the computer, files, and other tools of his trade as a historian. The books were almost entirely nonfiction and about American history. He read an occasional novel but mostly, as with *Law & Order,* his fiction reading was for enjoyment, distraction. For the most part, he found the stories of the real people of the American Revolution wilder and funnier and more exciting that those the novelists made up.

The framed photographs were of his mom and dad and his two younger brothers and their families, either at the folks' house in Connecticut or atop mountains, horses, Ferris wheels, or other vacation getaways. R occasionally regretted that he didn't have children. Still, he figured that someday he might, even if he had to marry a single mother to do it. Samantha had not been married before. She had no children. Never mind about Samantha. That's over. Goodbye, Samantha. Forget Samantha.

Gwinnett had written a cover letter, addressed to all three members of the committee, which said:

> *Here are "the goods." I suggest we have our call to resolve*
> *the matter as soon as possible. My assistant will be in*
> *touch to set up a time that is convenient for everyone.*
> *Cheers. John.*

What in God's name was there to cheer about?

"The goods."

There was a page-long SUMMARY OF FINDINGS from the research service. The meat was in the second paragraph.

Our search of *Ronald Reagan: The Last Founding Father* by Rebecca Kendall Lee produced a total of fifty-four Direct Instances. They break down as follows:

— Fourteen uses of one or more full and consecutive sentences from previously published works by other authors with no or only minor changes.
— Twenty-seven uses of near-identical phrases with five or more words from previously published works.
— Thirteen instances of similar phrasing with four or fewer identical word arrangements found in previously published works.

In addition, there were eighty-two indirect instances, where the material or idea was identical to previously published material but not in the form of an exact wording.

In every case, the previously published material was not in quotation marks or otherwise cited in the book as a direct use. While the original sources were listed at the end under a general bibliography, there was no mention of the fact that specific material from them was used in the book.

R turned to the backup material. There was a half-inch-high bound booklet of pages, each filled with matching citations that added up to what had been summarized. The format, eerily enough, followed that of those few terrible pages Rebecca had thrust on him about his *Post* op-ed piece.

He opened to pages and citations here and there, at random.

Page 133, *Dutch,* Edmund Morris:

"Finally he drove six hundred and sixty miles, until desert and sierra gave way to orange groves and the long Santa Monica highway, at the end of which the sun was setting, red with fatigue."

Page 77, Lee:

"Then he drove the final six hundred and sixty miles, until the desert and sierra surrendered to orange groves and the long Santa Monica highway at the end of which the sun was setting, dark red with weariness.'

Page 125, *Ronald Reagan,* Lou Cannon:

"The mini-memo was designed to play to Reagan's strengths and dodge his weaknesses. He was good at making decisions, which the mini-memo encouraged, and poor at doing his homework."

Page 14, Lee:

"The mini-memo was aimed at playing to Reagan's strengths and ducking his weaknesses. He was great at making decisions, which the small memo encouraged, but poor at doing his homework."

Page 105, *The Right Moment,* Matthew Dallek:

"On television he did not appear strident. But the skills for which he would later become so well known were not yet tested in early 1965."

Page 78, Lee:

"The television skills for which he would later become so famous were not developed in 1965 but, even so, he did not come over as strident."

Page 67, *What I Saw at the Revolution,* Peggy Noonan:

"Speechwriting was where the administration got invented every day. And so speechwriting was, for some, the center of gravity in that administration, the point where ideas and principles still counted."

Page 102, Lee:

"Speechwriting in the Reagan Administration was at the center—the core. That was where principles and ideas counted and where they became positions. It was where, on a daily basis, the administration got invented."

R read carefully through the entire array of citations. Some of them, particularly those like the Noonan one where the words were not identical, caused the heat to rise in R's body, anxiety in his soul. *Me?*

. . .

He went back out to the hallway, grabbed his small black canvas Tumi roller bag, and finally went upstairs. Now he would wash and change.

But before he could do more than take off his coat, shirt, and tie and switch on the shower, he remembered the telephone. He had not checked it for messages.

Gwinnett's secretary wanted to know if 5 P.M. Tuesday—today—would work for the conference call.

Samantha was "just checking in." No need to call back. "Hancock is still dead and I may be too, soon. The book's not working. Sorry about missing Wally's big goodbye." Her voice was subdued, sad—almost sweet.

There were two calls from friends who wanted to make lunch or dinner plans. Jack Hart of the *Post* thanked him for the Ben piece. *Your $300 check is in the mail.* R's brother Rich, a neat kid who worked as a fund manager on Wall Street, said he had to come to Washington late next month. What about a meal?

And there were the usual calls from people who offered opportunities to improve his security and fire protection in Georgetown or wanted to put him on a regular bottled water route.

The last call on the machine was from Harry Dickinson.

R, this is Harry, Harry Dickinson. I just got to Washington. I came solely to see you. I'm at the Four Seasons, just down the street from you. It's urgent that we talk. Call me now. I'm in room 809. You must be back home. Wally's girl—you know, Clara, the one with the legs and the ashes—said you left this morning. Call me, R. Urgent stuff, I promise.

NINE

The Garden bar on the lobby level of the Four Seasons Hotel was an arrangement of plants, tables, discreet lighting, and a piano player that R and Samantha often used as a meeting place when they first met. That was because real privacy was available, along with drinks and a variety of light things to eat.

R told the young woman hostess at the podium that he was meeting a man named Dickinson. When she hesitated, he quickly added, "He resembles a bush"—and she took him immediately to Harry, at a table against the east wall next to a plate-glass window that overlooked Rock Creek Parkway. No one was close enough to overhear anything they said.

Just over an hour had passed since R heard Harry's message on the answering machine. As he sat down across from the editor, the man at the piano began playing a song R liked, Henry Mancini's "Moon River" from the movie *Breakfast at Tiffany's*. R viewed the music as a good omen.

It wasn't.

"I went directly from that party yesterday afternoon to the BFU bookstore, where I bought copies of your two books," said

Harry, launching right into his urgent mission. His dark hazel eyes were beaming in a way R had never seen before.

He had barely said hello and seemed annoyed by the delay of a waiter taking R's order. Harry had a martini—straight up with three olives—sitting in front of him. Half of it was already gone. R asked for a glass of chardonnay and an order of pita bread and hummus.

"I began reading *Franklin at Craven Street* in the taxi on the way to the train station, and I continued with it and then on with *Ben and Billy* until I arrived back in New York. I finished it last night at my apartment. Why did nobody tell me about these books? You're a terrific writer, R, an artist of word and phrase, sentence and paragraph. Your words literally flow. And they do so uniquely—in a way that is identifiable as yours and yours alone."

R had always felt comfortable about his ability as a writer. But nobody, let alone somebody with the extraordinary credentials and experience of Harry Dickinson, had ever said anything like this to him—at least, not directly.

The waiter, a young Latino man in a short white coat and black pants, delivered R's wine and snack. But before R could touch either, Harry continued talking.

"I am a student and practitioner of the different ways writers use language. It's called style, of course, and I am what's called a style man—a Henry Higgins of writing style, you might say. I told someone once that I could tell the difference between sentences by Updike and Roth or McCullough and Morris at fifty yards. That's not bragging, that's just good reporting. Read me a sentence or two of just about any prominent work, past or present, fiction or nonfiction, and there's a damned good chance I can identify the writer."

R needed a very large gulp of his chardonnay, but his hand would not move toward the glass.

"So as I finished the last words of *Ben and Billy* I was most impressed. Then something began to gnaw at me. I said to myself, Harry, where have you read this style before? I then recalled a brief conversation I had with Bill Paine the day Wally died. Bill said Wally had granted every cent of the royalties from *Ben Two* to you, R. I had made the original arrangement with our royalty department, of course, for the fifty-fifty split. But now you, R, would get it all. That's a sizable flow of money; most likely it will last forever. That book, in hardback or paper, will never be out of print in your lifetime, either in English or in most other major languages. I thought it interesting at the time that he would give you half for *Ben Two* but nothing for *Ben One,* because I knew you were his researcher and helpmate on that first volume as well. Nothing from the first, half from the second—and then *all* from the second? I wondered."

R's interest in drinking and eating now gone, he looked over toward the parkway. It was dusk, rush hour, meaning all four lanes were open only one way—north out of the city, just as they all went south in the morning. Most of the cars had their headlights on, but he could recognize some of the car makes and models. Here came a Mercedes 230, a Honda, a BMW 122i, a Ford Taurus. When he was fourteen, he could recognize the make and model of any car, and he was still pretty good at it. Not as good as Harry Dickinson was at picking out writing styles, maybe, but pretty good.

"Then, very late last night, it all began to reveal itself to me. To refresh myself a bit, I took down *Ben Two* from my bookshelf. I have a copy of every book I've edited in my library at home. There are four hundred and seventy-four: all of them for Green Tree, all of them quality. Two-thirds nonfiction, one third fiction; that's the ratio I like to maintain. Eleven Pulitzers, eight National Book Awards. Not a bad record, if I do say so myself."

Harry paused, for one purpose only: for R to give some signal that Harry was not the only one who would say such a thing about his record.

R nodded and blinked. He had yet to say a word.

And Harry went on.

"Well, there was no question about it. The person who wrote *Ben Two* was the same one who wrote those two books of yours. Since it seemed most unlikely that Wally would go around writing books for you, that left only one possibility—one certainty, really. You, R Taylor, not Wally Rush, are the author of *Ben Two.*"

R put the glass of wine between his two hands and stared at it.

"I know it's true, R," said Harry. "It *is* a certainty. I am never wrong about things like this."

R said nothing.

"You remember how impressed I was with those first pages from *Ben Two?* I should have picked up on it then. You *do* remember, don't you, R? I talked about how terrific the writing was, how stunned I was that Wally could produce such terrific stuff."

R continued staring at his full wineglass. The hummus remained undisturbed; the pita slices were getting cold and stiff.

"I pretty much thought from the beginning, when I read those first few pages, that Wally probably had not written it," said Dickinson. "I gave a few moments to wondering who—maybe even you—was the real writer, but I couldn't allow myself to linger long on that, of course."

That got R's attention. *Of course? Why didn't you say something—do something—if you guessed Wally hadn't written the book?* That's what R was thinking. But he continued to hold his tongue—about everything.

"For the record, R," said Harry, "let's begin with your confirming you wrote *Ben Two.*"

R didn't even raise his eyes.

"I know it's true, but say it. Say, 'Yes, Harry, I wrote *Ben Two.*' I have a strong feeling it will be good for you. Say it, R. For your own sake."

R said nothing.

Harry was not a man who handled silences well. He waited only a few more seconds before going on. "I have a proposal. Definitely not a modest proposal. As a matter of fact, it is anything but modest. You want to hear it?"

R didn't want to listen to another word from Harry Dickinson. Not even a word of goodbye. He wanted to leave the Garden of the Four Seasons and return to his wonderful little house, to his wonderful little research on the early presidencies . . . and, yes, even to the awfulness of dealing with the Rebecca Lee problem and, even more, giving serious thought about what to do further about validating—dealing with—the papers in the cloak and the allegations not only of murder but even of statutory rape against Ben!

But his body would not move. He wanted to scoot out of his chair, stand, and walk away from this table, out of this bar and away from Harry.

R really did want to leave. He knew he *had* to.

Harry ended the silence again.

"You and I—maybe just you, depending on how you feel about it—have a news conference. Not here but in New York. You say, and I confirm from my own professional observations and judgments, that you are the real author of *Ben Two*. You tell the story—whatever the story is—of how you came to write that book for your late great friend and Franklin historian, Wallace Stephen Rush. I assume you did it out of sympathy and, in a way, as a form of tribute to this distinguished man of history and scholarship. You say that you plan to tell the full story in a book that will include other aspects to the ongoing rediscovery of growing appreciation for the mind and contributions of Benjamin Franklin. You say the title, in keeping with the tradition and in honor of Wally Rush, will be *Ben Three*."

Strength and movement were returning to R's legs.

"I know I can get you a healthy advance. But, more important, imagine your extraordinary gifts as a writer, brought to bear in telling this most extraordinary story of an acolyte's extreme loyalty to a diminished mentor resulting in the creation, by you, of a best-selling Pulitzer Prize–winning historical masterpiece. There would most likely be a move to take the *Ben Two* Pulitzer away from Wally posthumously and award it to you. Knowing you, I would guess that you would probably decline, insisting that it always remain Wally's. But it doesn't really matter which way that goes. Think about *Ben Three.* My heart, my whole being—as well as my parent multimedia company's bank account—leaps at the thought of its potential. There would be sales and prizes far beyond anything even *Ben Two* did. But besides that, R, you deserve the credit. Professionally, *Ben Two* belongs on *your* résumé, on *your* list of triumphs and accomplishments. It's simply not fair that Wally, bless his dear departed soul, be forever credited for a book he didn't write. It's not only immoral, it's unethical and maybe—who knows?—illegal. It's the ultimate form of plagiarism. Yes, that's correct. Of course, you wouldn't tell the story that way or come anywhere close to making that kind of allegation. For you, it was not plagiarism, it was creationism for a friend, a hero—"

R was on his feet and gone in the kind of quick, shifting, loping movement he hadn't used since he evaded the pass rush when playing quarterback for the Griswold High Tigers many years ago.

Harry threw some cash on the table and gave chase, yelling at R to stop, to at least talk to him.

But after a couple of blocks, Harry the Bush gave up. "I'll be in touch," he hollered at R, who did not look back.

. . .

He got a whiff of her perfume the second he stepped back inside the house. Then he heard her crying. He followed the fragrance and the sound into the kitchen.

Samantha was sitting on a stool at the small table next to the stove. Her head was down on her arms, on the table.

"Samantha, what's wrong?" R said, going to her. "What happened?"

She raised her head. Her beautiful face was wet with tears, twisted in agony and pain. Her nose was red from God knows how long this had been going on.

"I can't write, R," she sobbed, standing and reaching toward him. "I'm no writer!"

He took her in his arms and held her tight. Her small, soft body heaved back and forth against his. He was a foot taller, so her flowing brown hair was in his face—which he loved, because, as always, it was clean and smelled of shampoo. He stroked the back of her head with his right hand.

He knew this woman. He loved this woman. *Hello, Samantha!*

Soon, they were sitting on the couch in the study curled up together.

"I just can't make the words come out the way I want them to. I know what I want to say, but I can't put the words together to say it. They're too dense, too hard to understand, too academic, too stupid. When I couldn't compose in longhand *or* on the laptop, I talked into my tape recorder. You suggested that, and I thought I should try it; goodness knows, I'm verbal! But not complete-sentence complete-idea verbal. I talked and talked into that machine, and then played it back and it sounded like—well, lifeless gibberish. Incomprehensible, lifeless gibberish. A doctor writing a prescription for a hemorrhoid salve puts more life into his words. So does a waitress taking an order for a bacon cheeseburger, hold the onions. I just can't do it. And I know now that I never will be able to, either. Not the way I want, at least. I don't want to be just somebody who can write. I can't stand to be an ordinary writer. I want to write superbly. I want to write like you and Wally. I want people to say I write like a dream. I want people to laugh when I write a funny story, cry when it's a sad one. I want, I want . . . and I can't, I can't."

R had been through this lament with her once before. That was six months ago over just the simple act of signing a contract with the University of Massachusetts Press to write the Hancock book. She was confident of her information but had debilitating doubts about her ability to produce a worthy book. He had encouraged and even railed at her to at least give it a try. How would she ever really know until she forced her bottom on a chair long enough to see if she could do it?

R knew that he would sense when she wanted him to say something. She wasn't there yet. He just continued to pat, caress, hug, and kiss her while she talked.

"I thought for a full day it wasn't my fault. It was John Hancock's. I said to myself, R and Wally are right. He's not much, really. I thought maybe I was trying to take a nobody worth two pages and stretch him into somebody worth three hundred. A guy whose number one achievement was to sign his name larger than anybody else. He had nothing to do with writing the blessed Declaration of Independence or any of the incredibly important ideas that went into it. His wealth and position came from an inheritance. He was no Ben. No Jefferson or Washington or Madison. He wasn't even an Adams.

"By the way, the more I read about Hancock and his friends in Massachusetts, the more I got to liking Adams. I know what you Ben lovers think about him, but maybe you're wrong. Ben was no picnic either, as I don't have to tell you. Sometimes I think, in fact, that nobody has really figured him out yet—not even Wally.

"The other problem with Hancock was that I don't like him. He was a jerk. At least, that's what I got to thinking. Maybe I was imagining it. I knew I was in trouble when I couldn't talk to him. I remembered what you and Wally always said. Until you know your guy well enough to have a conversation with him—the way you said you did with Ben—you can't write about him. The more I knew about Hancock, the more I grew to despise him. So for a while I blamed him. *I can't write a coherent sentence because of you, John Hancock! You jerk!*"

Samantha looked up at R and smiled. R laughed out loud. He couldn't help himself. Samantha Louise Middleton was one very funny woman. Except when they were fighting, which unfortunately was much too often, or like a while ago when she was crying, just the sight of her made R grin. There was something about the flounce in her walk and her other movements, her salty language—picked up at home, she claimed, from an ex-marine father—and her very strongly delivered opinions that tickled him, lifted him.

That had been pretty much the case from their chance beginning. They happened to sit next to each other at an ARHA symposium on whether Jefferson really was the father of Sally Hemings's children. It was held in a meeting room at Georgetown University, where Samantha was an associate professor of Early American History. Out of professional curiosity, R simply walked over to the campus from his house to hear the discussion. There were experts of various kinds on the panel, and they were evenly split—two against two—on the validity of the DNA testing and other evidence. When the meeting broke up, R, not consciously on the make, said to the magnificent-looking woman on his left, "All this is another great lesson in the basic truth that history never ends." She agreed. They introduced themselves and exchanged current stations and interests in life. "I have always admired Dr. Rush and would give anything to meet him sometime," Samantha said. R remarked that Wally was, in fact, due in Washington in a couple of weeks for a meeting of some historical commission and he—R—would be delighted to arrange something. A few minutes later, he suggested that they continue this conversation at the bar at 1812, a restaurant just off campus. They had been mostly together ever since, and Samantha moved in with R nearly a year ago with a loose agreement to get married soon.

"Did you have your way with that Wally assistant the other night in Philadelphia?" she asked now.

"No, I did not."

"Maybe just a little intellectually based physical affection between Franklin scholars?"

"No!"

"Well, then, what did you do with her?"

R told her about what he ate for dinner at the Brasserie Perrier and the ceremony for Wally, with Clara being the one in charge of the ashes. He did not tell her that he had offered Clara a job or even about the proposed new institute. This was not the time. Right now, it was all about Samantha—and their future together.

"Do you honestly believe you can and will be faithful to me, R?" she said.

"How many times have we been through this?"

"You weren't at all faithful to your first two wives, were you?"

"Neither of them was you!"

And then, like a bell at the end of time on a TV quiz show, the telephone rang.

R moved to disentangle himself from Samantha.

"Let it ring," she said.

"I can't. It's a conference call about Rebecca Lee."

He picked up the telephone receiver on the desk with one hand and grabbed the FedExed Rebecca papers with the other. He tossed them to Samantha with accompanying body language that said to help herself to an interesting read.

"Yes, this is Taylor," he said into the phone, as he sat down at the desk. "Sure. I can go ahead now if everyone else can. . . . Let's go then. Hello, John . . . Sonya . . . Joe. Are you all there?"

They were all there.

.   .   .

"I have asked my chief assistant, Alexander Stockton, to join us—we call him Patrick around here, of course," said John Gwinnett. "Alex will make a verbatim transcript of what we say—and, possibly, decide—that can be forwarded to the ARHA office. I trust that meets with everyone's approval?"

There were no objections, just a smattering of hellos and acknowledgments to Stockton, who presumably was sitting somewhere in Williamsburg with John Gwinnett. Gwinnett's field was Patrick Henry, but R had no idea why Stockton would be called Patrick.

"Dr. Taylor, before proceeding, let me say that I thought the farewell events for Wally were perfect," Gwinnett said.

"I agree. Wally got a good sendoff," said R.

He glanced over at Samantha on the couch, still reading the Rebecca report. She looked up and rolled her eyes at him. He knew what she was saying with that: "The goods" were indeed the goods.

R wished he had had a chance to discuss with Samantha Rebecca's blackmail threat: Save me, R, or I take you down with me on phony charges. He had kept Rebecca's written charges and the specific *Gotcha!* threats. But there hadn't been an opportunity yet to show or tell her anything. So be it. He was on his own, and he hoped he knew exactly where he was going.

"I must say—just to begin the discussion—that it's about as open-and-shut a situation as I have ever encountered," Gwinnett said. "Shockingly so, if I may add that comment."

"Amen," said Sonya. Or at least R assumed it was Sonya. Her voice was so soft it was hard to tell. But she was the only female involved in this meeting.

"I agree, but I assume we will now give Rebecca Lee an opportunity to respond to these specific allegations?" It was Joe Hooper. No lynchings, please, remained his message.

There was silence for a count of two—three—four. R knew it was his turn to speak and everyone was waiting for him to do so. He was thinking. Joe Hooper had raised a good point. But so had John and Sonya.

"There can be no defense for such blatant plagiarism," Gwinnett said.

"Amen," said Sonya.

R had expected more words—more passion and force—from Sonya. Here, finally, she had in the crosshairs a person she detested, despised, abhorred. An enemy, politically and personally. Why was she only saying quietly to Gwinnett, "Amen"?

R decided to push her a bit. "*Amen* means what, exactly, in this context, Sonya?"

"That the evidence is strong."

"Stockton forwarded a full copy of the report to Dr. Lee as well as to each of you," said Gwinnett. "She knows the exact nature of the damning evidence against her."

"Yes, but, as Joe says, aren't we obligated to hear her defense, no matter how puny and insufficient it may be?" asked R.

He couldn't help noticing Samantha. She shook her head and then raised her right arm above as if it was holding a hangman's noose. She closed her eyes and slumped her head over to the side. *Hang her!*

R had to suppress a laugh.

"I believe we have no choice but to have a face-to-face meeting with her," Joe Hooper said firmly. "That is the only fair and responsible thing to do."

"I agree that we probably should, but I'll leave that to the rest of you to decide," mumbled Sonya.

There was an eerie silence on the conference-call line.

"What's wrong, Sonya?" R finally said.

"Nothing."

"Has she been after you?"

Sonya said nothing, and neither did anyone else for a few seconds.

"As a matter of fact, she actually threatened *me*," R said. There, he did it. He had not intended to say this, but there it was.

Samantha was off the couch. She came up behind him and put her arms around his neck and down onto his chest.

"Me too R," said Sonya, still barely audible. "She claimed she had evidence that I had stolen something in my first Abigail Adams book. I checked her citations. She's wrong. Yes, I read a lot of prior material, but I gave full credit and had everything directly quoted between quotation marks. She said she found a time or two when there could have been better attributions. I told her that was absurd. She told me to 'tell it to the judge'—a committee like our very own that she would insist be formed."

"That woman is dangerous," Gwinnett said.

Said Hooper, "I saw her in Philadelphia at the ceremony for Dr. Rush. All she said was that she sure did appreciate my speaking up for treating her fairly. I took it to be a bit of blatant—shall we say—caressing of a particular part of my anatomy."

"She came my way at Philadelphia but I walked away from her," said Gwinnett. "Even before I knew she was a first-class plagiarist, I knew she was a first-class fool for equating Reagan with the Founding Fathers."

R agreed with Gwinnett about the Reagan comparison, but he stayed on the real subject. "Rebecca's ammunition against me has to do with an op-ed piece in *The Washington Post* last week. I let some ideas from a twenty-five-year-old Timothy Morton essay linger too long in my brain before writing my piece. She admitted it wasn't anything serious but said I would be smeared anyhow in the process of trying to explain myself. Same as she said to you, Sonya. 'Tell it to the judge.' "

"This is an outrage!" yelled Gwinnett. "I say we throw everything we have at her!"

Again, there were a several beats of silence. No one joined in to shout, *Right on, John!* The clear unspoken message was, instead, *Maybe not so fast, John.*

Joe Hooper finally said, "As a matter of fact, what is the 'everything' we can actually throw?"

R had wondered that a time or two himself in the last few days. But with so much else going on in his life, he hadn't bothered to check any ARHA booklets or ask anyone.

Gwinnett said, "We can recommend the ARHA censure her publicly—condemn her and her actions in strong words shouted from housetops. We can urge her university or college employer to reprimand or even dismiss her. We can urge her publisher to withdraw the book in question from print. We can ask that any awards or prizes she may have received for the book be rescinded. And we can strip away her membership in the ARHA"

Hooper was the first to laugh. "Except for the public accusations, that's pretty much nothing."

"That's true," said Sonya. "She doesn't teach anymore, for one thing. And I can't believe that awful Reagan book won anything but a kiss from a right-wing book club."

"Her publisher might defend her—and love the publicity," R added, his mind targeted on Harry Dickinson's conduct and example.

"Then it boils down to a confrontation," said Gwinnett, remaining very much in charge. "I am still unable to travel because of my knee, so that will make it necessary for us to meet here in Williamsburg. Is that a problem for anyone?"

No one had an objection. R, for his part, considered visits to the historic area of Colonial Williamsburg to be the single most pleasurable part of his life as an eighteenth-century historian. There were many sites to study American history, but CW was the only one where one could sense, feel, and experience it. There was nothing he enjoyed more than strolling the streets, sipping a cup of apple cider, listening to the music from the taverns, exchanging exaggerated greetings with the interpreters, in their eighteenth-century dress, and trading exaggerated dialogue with the several skilled actors who regularly portrayed such major colonial figures as Thomas Jefferson and Patrick Henry.

"I will have Dr. Lee contacted to pursue possible dates with her and with each of you and then firm up the arrangements," said Gwinnett. "I must give some thought to what would be the most suitable Williamsburg setting for the occasion."

"Let's put her in the stocks alongside the old courthouse," Sonya said, in full voice.

. . .

They went for a walk, going out to 31st Street and then left two blocks up to R Street, west by the famous Oak Hill Cemetery and Montrose Park toward Dunbarton Oaks and Wisconsin Avenue.

Neither looked at much of anything on either side of the street. Mostly Samantha was listening to R recount the events that led up to the Rebecca conference call. She had only heard his end of the conversations up to now and had paid very little attention to R's ARHA committee assignment, except to blindly defend Rebecca because she was a woman.

When he finished, Samantha said, "I'm sorry about what I said on the phone the other day. That was uninformed, stupid, silly. If there was capital punishment for plagiarists, Rebecca deserves the rope—or the needle; whatever. Fried, even."

They crossed Wisconsin and continued walking west through a row of fairly new town houses. R pointed to one. "Somebody told me Meg Greenfield lived in that one." Greenfield had been the editor of the *Washington Post* editorial page and a *Newsweek* columnist before her death a few years ago. She was a good friend of Mrs. Graham, once her neighbor down R Street.

"Question," said Samantha. "Did you intentionally buy that house of yours because it was close to R Street?"

"I thought you'd never ask."

"It only now just struck me."

"The answer is no. I loved the house and the neighborhood. It's possible that its faint Georgian resemblance to Ben's old house on Craven Street had an effect too."

"You should tell people that R Street is named after you."

R laughed. Maybe now was a good time to bring up John Hancock and Samantha's writing problem. He wanted to know more about the specifics, the particular scenes or insights or what-evers that were causing her trouble.

She waved him off with a friendly but tight "I'm not ready to talk about that" and brought the subject back to him. Was anything else exciting or monumental going on his life besides the Rebecca drama and, of course, the death of Wally?

"Not really," he said. It was a reflex answer. He wasn't quite ready to bring Samantha into any of his other truly monumental crises: the Eastville papers, *Ben Two* and the possible Three, or even running a Wally-Ben center at BFU. He had been thinking about telling her everything. He knew he needed some counsel, some wisdom, some reactions—some help. And to his mind at this moment, there was nobody else but Samantha from whom he could get it. He was almost ready—but not yet. She also really did have to deal with her Hancock problem.

They had been holding hands. Now he put his left arm around her shoulders and pulled her to him. "Speaking of names as we were a moment ago, I assume you're not planning to take my last name?"

She stopped, twisted away, and look up at him. "Do you really still want to marry me?"

"Yes."

"Why? Please tell me why?"

"Because I love you—enough even to stay faithful to you."

She moved back under his arm. Without another word, they turned around as one and hurried back to his house.

.   .   .

Afterward, still in bed and sipping chardonnay R had poured for them, they would talk some more about marriage and their lives together. Maybe, thought R, he might even bring up one or more of his other crises.

That thought reminded him that while he had checked his mail and his telephone answering machine, he had not booted up his computer and gone through any e-mail that might have come since he left for Philadelphia.

When was that anyhow? This is Tuesday. Wally died last Thursday. Good God almighty! Look at all that has happened to me—look at all the trucks that have hit me—in just five goddamn days!

With Samantha's permission, he detoured into the study to his desktop.

There was only one e-mail of consequence. It was from Clara Hopkins in Philadelphia.

r, dear boss:

no record of either a roger or "button" nelson in colonial census, medical, military, or tax records. nothing about either in any newspaper from the time. thinking of other places to look. are you sure they existed?

some good information on melissa anne harrison wolcott: born here in 1744, daughter of prominent Quaker family. married jonathan david wolcott in 1763, had four children. died in

philadelphia in 1794. all of this confirmed from more than
one source.

now will you tell me why you wanted to know this stuff?

hope all is well. look forward to your return.

your obedient servant,
clara h.

R, with a pencil on a notepad, did some fast adding and sub-
tracting.

The Melissa Anne Harrison Wolcott in Clara's records could
not be the same one in the Eastville papers or in Johnny Rutledge's
records. She would have been twenty-two years old when Ben met
her, and already married. And she would have still been alive years
after Ben supposedly hired the Nelsons to kill her.

A Prophecy situation after all?

But what about Carter Hewes's fairly solid take on the dating
of the pages and the writing? Unless they were a forgery. Joshiah
Ross and his cloak certainly were real. Johnny Rutledge seemed
sure about his data on Melissa Anne Harrison being a kid too. Unless. . . .

What now? What next? There was so much of this to check
and recheck. There was also the farmhouse meeting. Is it even possible that Adams, Washington, Hamilton, and Madison, as well as
Ben, could have conceivably gathered on that particular day in
1788? Their diaries and personal papers should be able to pinpoint where each man was on that date.

He chose not to discuss any of this with Samantha. So, once
in bed, they talked about getting married: possible wedding dates,
locations, size and style. Samantha said she'd call her mother in

Kansas tomorrow. Her father, the marine she claimed had taught her how to cuss, had died two years earlier of lung cancer.

"This is the number-one wedding for me—and for my mom and my family," said Samantha. "You've had some practice."

R acknowledged that simple truth. His first wedding, to a wonderful woman who was meant to live with a Wall Street broker rather than a historian, took place on a small mountainside near Great Barrington, just a few miles over the line in Massachusetts from his Connecticut hometown. Two hundred people came in dark suits and long dresses, danced to a large orchestra, ate and drank well, and were merry under a large white tent. Trish had hated life in Philadelphia as the wife of a graduate assistant. Fortunately, there were no children.

His second wedding with a Methodist preacher friend officiating, was held in his own Philadelphia living room with only a few other friends present. Maggie, also a wonderful woman, loved campus life and its professors, instructors, and graduate assistants. She had trouble being with only one at a time. Fortunately, there were no children with Maggie either.

In both marriages, R had made his own major contributions to their failure. That was mostly because of his own inability to remember he was married when the young coeds and Clara Hopkinses of his work world made themselves obviously available. Samantha, within days of meeting R at that Jefferson symposium, had learned through the small Early American historian grapevine of R's two soured marriages and of his reputation. At the time she had said often that, based on his record, she didn't trust him but she couldn't resist him.

She didn't say it now, of course. They had moved past all that to Why not have the wedding in Wichita? On the other hand, Samantha now had more friends here on the East Coast than she did in Kansas....

R was barely listening. Since reading Clara's e-mail, his mind had been slamming with thoughts about Ben and the cloak and the papers, the murder and child sex charges, and the extraordinary trial in a Pennsylvania farmhouse. He felt a sudden intense need to get away—not just from Washington and this town house but the Ben papers and all of the rest. He needed to be in another location, another space, another environment to work everything out.

He sprang straight up in bed.

"Craven Street!" he announced.

"What about it?" Samantha responded with some alarm. "I'm not about to get married in an old house in London—"

"No, no. Not that. Let's go there."

"On our honeymoon? You've got to be kidding."

"Tomorrow. Let's go tomorrow. We'll stay at the Savoy, around the corner. Just for a day or two."

Samantha was now also sitting straight up.

"Take your laptop," R said. "We'll work on your writing problem. I'll take some stuff I need to do too."

"What stuff? You already did that Ben-at-Craven-Street book, remember? You told me you spent days, weeks there. Now it's about the early presidency. Repeat after me: 'I am now working on the early presidency, none of which happened anywhere near Craven Street.' "

He leaped out of bed.

"Where are you going?" she asked.

"To the computer. I'll see what Expedia and the others have for tomorrow. Who knows, last-minute can sometimes turn up very cheap airline fares. Same for the Savoy."

He had stopped at the door.

"Aren't you even going to ask if I want to go—if I *will* go?" Samantha said.

"I'm sorry—"

"I have to go back up to Pennsylvania and give that asshole

John Hancock one more try. I really do. Maybe I can get him into a conversation—"

"I understand."

She sighed. In a soft, quiet voice, she asked, "Why, R? Why, dearest one of all, do you want to go back to Craven Steet?"

"To talk to Ben—again."

TEN

R hoped it was late enough in the morning for Ben's house to be open. He had taken the early overnight United flight from Washington Dulles, arriving at London Heathrow just after 6:30 A.M. But with the deplaning, waiting for luggage, getting a taxi ride to the West End and all the rest, it was now almost ten o'clock. His hotel room on the seventh floor of the Savoy, a so-called deluxe bedroom he booked through an Internet discounter for $375 a night, had fortunately been ready early. It had a king-sized bed, a marble-floored bathroom and 24-hour butler service, none of which R had paid any attention to before heading out the door for the elevator.

In less than five minutes he was downstairs, through the lobby, and out onto the Strand, the busy avenue of commerce and show business that parallels a curvaceous bump in the Thames. It serves as a kind of man-made dividing line between the Embankment leading southward down to the river and Covent Garden and the major West End theater district to the north.

R turned left, went five blocks, and made another left at a side alley to Craven Street. It was a cool gray London morning and he was still in the blue blazer, open-collared cotton sport shirt, and khaki chinos he had worn on the plane. But he was too excited to notice whether he was hot or cold.

There was the house, 36 Craven Street, on the left side of the street. Of all the places Ben had lived during his long and illustrious life, including another house here on Craven Street, this was the only one that still survived.

The restoration work on the outside had clearly been completed. The narrow three-story Georgian brick town house looked fixed—gentrified—as did those around it. The last time R had been here there was still scaffolding on the outside and a mess within. An organization of mixed British and American sponsorship had raised the money and the energy to bring 36 Craven Street back to what it was when Ben lived there. The plans were for tours, archives, study centers. They already staged seminars and other functions and put out a publication called *The Craven-Street Gazette* patterned after a similar fun paper Ben published when he lived here. Both Wally and R had participated in fundraising and various educational events. R had also joined the Friends of Benjamin Franklin House and had contributed $500 a year for the last five years.

The place looked absolutely perfect from the outside. There were the three lines on a 24-by-16-inch brass plaque:

BENJAMIN FRANKLIN
(1706–1790)
LIVED HERE

There was fresh black paint on the iron railings around the lower outside steps to the basement entrance and the alcove window on the main floor above. That was the window of the parlor where

Ben often took his strange air baths, as well as entertaining, reading, and observing the passing people, animals, and conveyances below on Craven Street.

R now did as Ben did; he looked down toward the Thames.

In a peculiar mind flip, R's thoughts went not to the real history of this street, which he knew so well from his own book's research. They jumped instead to the six Benjamin Franklin mystery novels written in the last few years by Robert Lee Hall, *Benjamin Franklin Takes the Case* being the first. Totally made up, of course, each is told in first-person mode by Nicolas Handy, Ben's fictional twelve-year-old illegitimate son. Nick serves as a kind of stenographer for the great man, and it is Nick's written records of Ben's excursions into solving murders and other dastardly London crimes that, according to the fictional preface, surfaced in 1987 among the papers of a Nick Handy descendant.

Art imitating life, truth told only in fiction, and similar clichés were foremost in R's thoughts at the moment. The possible parallels, real or imagined, between Nick Handy's stories and those in the twelve Eastville papers were inescapable. And possibly meaningless. And irrelevant. And stupid. Unless . . .

But it all seeped into R's mind nevertheless, as did what Nick said about Craven Street in one of the books. "The street was a pleasant one, with much rattling traffic." Ben's house was "part of a row of brick terrace houses sloping gently toward a timber yard by the Thames" fifty yards away. On the river were "rowboats and wherries" along with fishermen with nets on "the gray-green waters."

Craven Street was a piece of real history, beyond the fact that Ben once lived here. There were some thirty structures that came right up to the sidewalks on both sides of the street. The timber yard at the end of Craven Street was long gone. Now there was a tiny park and then Embankment Road, a major four-lane thoroughfare that followed the course of the Thames in both directions for several miles. Craven Street itself, now paved and marked neatly for permit parking only, was mostly dirt in Ben's time. Ben's carriage, driven by Peter, his freed-slave servant, often threw up dust or mud as it sped off on one of Ben's many diplomatic, and social—or detective—missions. R knew this from the scores of historical resources he plumbed in researching his own book about Franklin in London.

"You had quite a life here, Ben," R said. Without thinking he spoke the words out loud. Then he looked around to see if anyone could have heard him and decided a nut was loose this morning.

There were only two or three people nearby, well-dressed men in suits and ties with umbrellas and briefcases, seemingly on their way to the tube or to offices. None showed any sign of having seen or heard something unusual. Did unshaven Americans in rumpled clothes often come here to Craven Street in the morning to speak aloud to Benjamin Franklin?

The first time R visited Craven Street was with Maggie twelve years ago, while on a European summer vacation. They came at Wally's strong urging, on the grounds that this was where Ben had lived for fifteen years—except for one brief break, almost continuously from 1757 to 1775—during a most important time in his life. To know Ben, you had to know Craven Street, Wally said. That initial trip led to seven more and to R's writing *Franklin at Craven Street*.

The book told the story of how Ben was here officially as the representative to His Majesty's government of Pennsylvania and eventually of other American colonies. His original purpose was to persuade the King and Parliament—anybody—to force the greedy descendants of the great William Penn, technically the owners of Pennsylvania, to submit to taxation just like all other citizens of the colony. Ben failed at that specific task, an outcome that left him and the Penns bitter enemies for life. But in the process, he came to represent to most Britons what was both good and bad about the rambunctious and ultimately rebellious American colonies. R's book also touched on Ben's personal life, which included his scientific experiments, social escapades, and intellectual pursuits.

Ben never owned the place. He was a boarder of Mrs. Margaret Stevenson, a widow who, with her daughter Polly, provided room, food and companionship, and eventually love and devotion for Ben. But there was no hanky-panky that R and other serious Ben scholars ever bought. Ben was indeed an appreciator of women, but he didn't manifest his appreciation with each in the same way. Polly Stevenson was eighteen when Ben first came to live on Craven Street with her and her mother. There is no recorded allegation, much less a confirmation, that Ben ever even made a pass at her. Theirs was a father-daughter relationship.

"Tell me about Melissa Anne Harrison, Ben," R said aloud, his eyes now on the parlor windows.

"It's open only occasionally for visitors, I rather think, sir," somebody said. The somebody was a male with a British accent. R, startled, turned to see a man in his late thirties standing next to him, also looking across the street at 36 Craven Street. He was in a dark-blue striped suit, white spread-collar shirt, and dark-blue-and-white polka-dot tie, an umbrella in one hand, a leather briefcase in the other.

"Thank you . . . right, I know. Thank you," R mumbled.

"Practicing your questions, I guess, then?" said the man, lifting his umbrella in a sign of adieu as he walked on.

R nodded and raised his right hand to give a wave to the man but stopped before doing so.

Instead, he waited another few seconds and walked across the street to the front door of 36 Craven Street.

It was time to get on with it.

. . .

A young woman answered R's knock. She appeared to be less than thirty, probably an American.

"Good morning," said R. He was set to go on immediately with a short spiel of introduction but she interrupted him.

"I am so sorry, sir, but we are not yet prepared to handle drop-in visitors," she said with a pleasant smile and an accent that R placed as Midwest, probably Chicago.

"I'm R Taylor—"

"*The* R Taylor?"

"Well, I guess—"

"Yes! You're R Taylor! Oh, my God!" The woman threw open the door. "I can't believe it's you!"

If R hadn't known better, he would have thought he was a rock star.

It seemed for a split second that she might actually grab him. But no. She stepped aside, and he went through the door into the front hallway.

"*Franklin at Craven Street* is my single most favorite book about Dr. Franklin," bubbled this most incredible young person—possibly, R thought at that moment, his single most favorite young person in the whole world. "The stories you told about that man and this house, and the way you told them—well, they are truly superb. I loved *Ben and Billy* too. You're a beautiful writer, Dr. Taylor."

She extended her right hand to him. He wanted to devour it.

You are a beautiful person, young lady. You are an intelligent, discerning, brilliant human being—among the very finest of your species.

That's what he thought. "Thank you, so much," was what he said. "You have certainly made my day."

Closer up now, he saw that her dark-blond hair was too long, her nose was slightly too large, and her skin was too rough, and as she escorted him away from the door he noticed that both her rear and her legs were slightly on the bulky and bowed side. But none of that mattered. Her beauty was in her mind, her judgment. Oh, yes. She had just provided for R an experience that seldom happens to historians and only occasionally to writers of any kind of books. John Grisham might get this treatment at a lawyers' convention, but that's about it.

Stephanie Thornton. That's what she now said her name was. She said it nervously, awkwardly.

She also quickly explained that the director, the curator, and the other staff members were away in Bath at a historical properties meeting. Only she and some of the restoration craftsmen were present.

"Everyone is going to be so upset that they missed you," she said.

"All I really need is to see the parlor. I understand the restoration there is the farthest along," R said, when she finally asked why he had come.

She made a sound that closely resembled that of a purring kitten.

"You're right about the parlor," she said. "We've already put furniture in there, so it's pretty much back the way it was when Dr. Franklin lived here."

She offered to take him through the entire house, but he declined. He had already been in every corner of the place, including the third floor, where, in Ben's time, Peter and the other servants slept, and to the second floor, where the two Stevenson women had their bedrooms. Ben's bedroom and the room he used for his scientific experiments were on the main floor behind the parlor.

They were actually standing at the entrance to the parlor now.

Stephanie's face lost some of its buoyancy. She clearly wanted to do something for him, to show him more.

"The basement," he said. "Take me to the basement, where they found the bones."

Once again, she appeared to be on the verge of grabbing him. But she resisted and said, "Follow me." The woman seemed truly excited.

The steps down were narrow, still under repair but not dangerous.

At the bottom, immediately in front of where the steps ended, was the kitchen.

"That's where Mrs. Stevenson prepared those marvelous meals for Dr. Franklin, and his son, William, and the many, many visitors of importance who came to this house."

R only smiled, and she led him to the basement room where the bones were found.

"I assume you know the whole story, Dr. Taylor?" she asked, and continued without waiting for an answer. "It was about three years ago. They were doing some archaeological excavation and—lo and behold!—they came across some bones buried below-ground here in the cellar."

Yes, young lady, thank you. R had followed the story closely. The local coroner of Westminster determined the bones to be from at least ten different people, all of eighteenth-century vintage. There was some initial concern and mischief over how they might be connected to Ben, but the mystery was quickly solved. A doctor named William Hewson married Polly Stevenson in 1770 and came to live at 36 Craven Street. He set up an anatomy laboratory in the basement, where he taught medical students how to cut up cadavers. The modern-day investigators concluded that Hewson, rather than throwing out the remnants of his work, simply buried them on the premises. One of the grocery store tabloids in the United States had run a full-page story under the headline:

BENJAMIN FRANKLIN SHOCKER!
He was a Founding Father, a signer of
the Declaration of Independence
—AND A SERIAL KILLER!

Nobody else picked up on that nonsense, and the episode moved quickly to focus on the history of surgery in Britain in the eighteenth century.

Stephanie pointed toward a spot in the corner, now covered with loose boards. "That's where the bones were found," she said. "Some irresponsible people went as far as to suggest the bones were evidence that Dr. Franklin might have been involved in murder. Can you imagine anything more ridiculous?"

R said he couldn't.

They went back upstairs, and Stephanie left him in the parlor, after R said he'd appreciate some time to simply sit there by himself.

.   .   .

"It's me, R Taylor, Dr. Franklin. Do you remember me?"

Ben said nothing.

There he sat between two of the parlor windows in a high-back Windsor chair covered in dark red fabric.

He was naked.

His legs were crossed, but otherwise only his eyes were unexposed. He was wearing a pair of silver-rimmed bifocals—Franklin Splits, they were called by most people after his death, in the mistaken belief that he had invented them rather than simply made them popular.

His was a physique of bulges. Some were made by muscles in his huge arms and hands and in the calves and thighs of his legs, but others—in his hefty midsection, breasts, and under his chin— were most likely fat. What else could be expected of a man already

seventy years old, particularly one who enjoyed few things more
than a good meal here at Craven Street or elsewhere with people
who shared his curiosities and interests.

*I was about to take an air bath. They are far superior to water
baths, in my opinion. My use of them sometimes sets the ladies of
Craven Street all a-twitter, but such is the price one pays for cleans-
ing oneself one's own way. I would prefer they be set a-glitter. Alas,
that is no longer to be.*

R was sitting on the floor directly across the room. Ben and his
air baths were part of the Ben mythology, a part, like so many others, that was based on fact. R knew Ben often began his days, no
matter the temperature, standing at one of these parlor windows
bathing his body in the cold morning air. Mrs. Stevenson suggested that he halt the practice in the name of modesty but to no
avail.

So it was no problem for R now to see Ben naked in the chair,
although he had been mostly clothed in their earlier conversations
when R was researching his Craven Street book.

The Craven Street restoration folks had done a super job here
in the parlor. The three large-framed floor-to-ceiling windows that
faced out onto Craven Street had been left unobstructed. There
was a stand-up desk against the wall between two of them, a tall
grandfather clock and chairs between and away from the others.
To Ben's right was the man-high fireplace with built-in bookshelves on both sides, over which hung a painting of knights on
horses. On the floor was a square rose and off-white patterned rug,
fifteen by fifteen feet. A small round table with another chair was
opposite Ben on the other side of the fireplace. All of the furnish-
ings were, to R's trained eye, authentic to the eighteenth century.

He would have had no trouble imagining men of science, politics, and the arts sitting here with a fully dressed Ben, playing chess,

listening to him play music on his handmade glass armonica, or discussing the origins of electricity, the heat lost from open fire-places, the true cause of the warmth in the Gulf Stream, and the urgent need to repeal the Stamp Act and later the Townshend Acts, two legislative moves by the British government that were pushing the American colonies toward rebellion. . . .

But that was not what he wanted to say this morning.

"Was Melissa Anne Harrison, later Wolcott, the mother of William?" R asked Ben.

I have never spoken of that subject, and I will not do so now.

"Why not?"

It could do harm to the woman involved.

"She is as long gone now as you are."

Some of us never are gone.

"I asked you before but I do so again: Didn't William have a right to know from whose womb he came?"

No.

"Why not?"

Because he was a traitor to his father and to his country.

"Did you know a woman named Melissa Anne Harrison, later Wolcott?"

No.

"Did you not see her on visits to her family home? Her father, Arthur Harrison—was he not a prominent Quaker businessman of your time and an acquaintance of yours?"

Many prosperous Quaker businessmen in the Philadelphia of my time who were my acquaintances.

"So you didn't know him or his family—most particularly a daughter named Melissa Anne?"

I think I have already answered that question. Move on, please. I'm getting a bit of a chill.

"I can wait while you dress, sir, if you'd like."

No, you may not wait. What else is on your mind?

"Did you have William's mother killed?"

That is an absurd and insulting question. Remember to whom you are speaking, young man.

"What is the answer, sir?"

Certainly not. In fact, I provided sums for her throughout her life.

"Was William's mother Melissa Anne Harrison Wolcott?"

How many times do I have to answer the same question?

"Did you know a man named Button Nelson in Philadelphia?"

The only buttons I have ever met were those on my clothing and that of others.

"You did not pay Button Nelson to murder Melissa Anne Harrison Wolcott?"

No, I did not.

"His brother Roger says you did."

I would have thought any brother of a button would have been a hole, not a Roger.

"You are not taking me seriously, sir."

Why should I?

"Because your reputation from this point on in history could depend on it."

How would you describe my reputation now?

"Excellent, really—and getting better all of the time."

Why is that?

"You are finally receiving the credit and admiration you deserve. George Washington and Thomas Jefferson, and recently John Adams, have, always received more serious attention as Founding Fathers than you."

Washington was a statue, Jefferson a pose, Adams a tree stump.

"What about Madison?"

A peacock. But a special peacock—to me, at least.

"Special in what way? I would have thought the differences

between the two of you in personality as well as on the issues would have precluded—"

He had occasion to see me through a difficult situation, and he did so.

"What situation, if I may ask?"

You may ask and I may choose not to answer, which I now do.

"What about John Hancock?"

A figure.

"What do you mean?"

Figure as in what goes with a head.

"My fiancée is writing a book on him now. She's having trouble doing so."

Tell her to write an aphorism about him instead.

"Why?"

An aphorism can be as short as one sentence.

"Such as?"

A man who signs his name large is a man who thinks small.

"Was there an informal trial of you on charges of murder and other related crimes before a jury of your peers: Washington, Hamilton, Madison, Adams?"

Impossible.

"Impossible?"

They were not my peers.

"You think awfully well of yourself, sir."

No man who does not think well of himself can do well.

"I have seen written evidence to indicate that you were . . . intimate . . . with a girl of thirteen—possibly even twelve—and that the girl was, in fact, Melissa Anne Harrison."

Do you believe it, in fact, to be true?

"I don't know yet."

When will you know?

"I don't know that either."

That is what you mean about damaging my place in history?

"Yes, sir."

What else?

"That this girl gave birth to William and later, when she was forty-five years old and on the verge of telling the world about her motherhood, you had her killed. That's what the Pennsylvania trial was about."

I told you there could be no such trial. Why would I have done what you have read that was charged against me?

"You were ill, already over eighty years old, and you wished to depart this world with your place in scientific, revolutionary, and intellectual history unsullied by charges that you impregnated a twelve-year-old girl and then later, when she was a mature woman, had her murdered in cold blood."

How many people know of these charges against me?

"As we speak, probably only one—me."

Are you going to tell anyone else, after we speak?

"I am a historian. If I believe they are true, I have no choice."

A man with no choices is no man.

"Is that from *Poor Richard's Almanack*?"

Have you read my essay on chess? Maybe it came from that. But, no matter, it is from Life itself. Choices are Life. Life is choices. I choose to play a game of chess, you choose to play a game of bowls. I chose revolution, my son William chose capitulation. I, you, he, she, we. They are personal pronouns; they are the beginnings of all sentences of action—of choice. Life choices are what make us different from the mongrels and the geese. The mongrel must fight and snarl; we can choose to do so or not do so. The geese must fly a certain direction at certain times of the year. We have no such musts. We are a species of choice. Some say it is God who put the possibility and luxury of choice in us; I say it matters less where it came from than that we recognize it as our Essence, our Power, our Force, and use it with gusto and purpose.

"So what should I do?"

You did not hear me, did you? Choices are all individual. Groups make choices as the result of individual agreements. No man can make another man's choices for him.

"You wrote rules for the game of chess and many other endeavors. Are there rules for choices?"

Ah, yes, indeed, and they are simple and as follows: No matter the will and the wit that goes into each, it is not possible to make nothing but perfect choices. Choices of expectation, of deduction, and even of love must find their way to final judgment through many outside forces beyond our control. Only choices of Honor are free of uncertainties. That is because they spring from and depend solely upon what comes from within.

"Thank you, sir. I've asked you this before—but one more time, Dr. Franklin. Whoever the mother was, why did she give you William to raise instead of keeping him herself?"

The answer to that question will be found in the Almanack.

"Where?"

Under, "A man who noses into another man's business soon no longer has a nose to nose."

"Yes, but what is to prevent one man from making a clear and free personal choice to so nose into the other man's business?"

Nothing except the risk of losing his nose.

"Thank you, sir."

You are welcome.

.   .   .

As he left 36 Craven Street a few minutes later, R felt foolish. Only a complete idiot would have come all this way to have an imaginary conversation with Ben—with anyone. Wally's conversation/mantra aside, it was a silly, stupid, childish thing to do.

What is such an exercise anyhow other than a make-believe recycling of what the imagining one in the conversation—the imaginer—already knows or suspects?

Unless, of course, one really believes in ghosts of historical figures past. . . .

R pled a personal emergency to the Savoy and United Airlines and was on his way back to Heathrow less than an hour later without having unpacked or even put his head on a hotel room pillow.

Yes, coming here to talk to Ben had definitely been a waste of his mind as well as his time, money, and energy.

Although Ben's line about Madison was arousing. What "difficult situation" did Madison see Ben through?

That phrase must have arisen from something R came across in his real Ben research. It would have had no meaning at the time but stuck in his mind until it came out of Ben's imagined mouth. That must be it.

ELEVEN

In the taxi from Dulles, R made two calls on his cell phone.

The first was to Jack Hart, the deputy editorial page editor of *The Washington Post.* Jack had been the one who handled R's op-ed page piece on Ben; without hesitation, he agreed to meet R at the *Post* in the morning at ten. All R had said was that it was urgent, to which Jack had replied, "Isn't everything—but sure, come ahead."

The other call was to Wes Braxton at the Eastern Pennsylvania Museum of Colonial History.

R began with the story he had roughed out on the plane. It was a lie but a small one, designed to buy some time and possibly much more, if necessary.

"Wes, about those papers from the cloak. I've had them checked for age and the like, and they certainly do appear to be authentically eighteenth century. There seems little question of that."

"I'm delighted to hear it," said Braxton, "although not surprised. The chain of possession on the cloak was right on that path."

R said, "Mmm, yes. Further examination also confirms my cursory reading for content the other day when I was with you. They appear to be someone's notes—or diary—as I had suspected."

"Somebody from the eighteenth century, for sure, then? Joshiah Ross, the guy who originally bought the coat?"

"Almost for sure, yes. But there appears to be no coherent message or story. The mention of murder and things like that are in apparent reference to somebody having seen it in a dream or otherwise imagined it."

"What about those initials that seemed to be referring to Benjamin Franklin—and maybe other Founding Fathers?"

"We were able to trace most of those initials to other people and meanings."

"That's a disappointment," said Braxton. "I was hoping that they would turn out to be something of real value."

So far so good—with the small lies.

"There's no reason for disappointment, Wes. I am pretty sure they would have great value in the antiquities market for serious private collectors of eighteenth-century American memorabilia."

"You think so?"

"I'm almost certain. I have come across many such people in my work. A lot of money changes hands for authentic examples of colonial life—such as these papers."

There was a brief silence. Clearly, Wes Braxton was doing exactly what R wanted him to do. He was considering.

"When you say 'a lot of money' what could we be talking about? God knows we need money at our place, as I told you. A little infusion of cash might be exactly what the doctor—and my future—ordered."

Now it was R's turn to consider—or at least continue the thinking he had already done about how high a price to throw out. How much would it take to get Braxton's attention and support?

"It's only an estimate," said R finally, "but it could go as high as fifteen thousand—possibly seventeen five."

"You don't mean the cloak too, do you? We couldn't sell that under any circumstances."

"No, no. Just the twelve sheets of paper."

There was quiet. The taxi was near the end of the two-lane section of Glebe Road, in the lane for crossing Chain Bridge into the District.

"Obviously, I would have to run this past our board and the Ross family heirs."

"Do you want me to make inquiries within the collectors' crowd to measure interest?"

"Would you do that? I hate to ask you to perform as a kind of broker in this."

"It's not a problem. I don't mind."

It's not a problem. I don't mind.

The call ended with the promise from each to get back to the other with an update when either had new information.

Then, once he was home, R sent an e-mail to Clara Hopkins in Philadelphia.

clara:

i need your help on another "small" item. could you determine the whereabouts on September 7, 1788, of ben, adams, hamilton, madison, and washington? i would love exact place and activity if possible. the information should be available for each through diaries and their own personal letters. i would suggest beginning with the databases at the libraries that house their respective papers—madison's at the university of virginia, hamilton's at columbia university, adams's at the massachusetts historical society. we should have that information on ben right there in wally's files but, if not, his

papers are at yale. the library of congress and the national
archives are the places to go for washington. you probably
already know all this and, if so, forgive me.

thanks.

r

She responded in less than a minute.

dear r big boss:

yes, sir. i will do what i can. it may not be quite as simple as you
suggest. but we'll see. again, i guess it's too much for you to
accompany the request with some word on WHAT IN THE HELL
IS GOING ON?

when are you coming back to philadelphia? an assistant of
some kind in elbow's office called this morning to inquire. she
said the president would like a word with you about an
important matter.

i wouldn't mind speaking to you myself. and, yes, of course, i
already knew where the papers of the founding fathers are kept.
i do not forgive you. but, for now, i remain your obedient servant,

clara

Elbow?
R answered:

tell elbow's office—and you—that i may be back in
philadelphia tomorrow. probably early afternoon. thanks again.
and i'm sorry again.

. . .

R laid out the two articles on Jack Hart's desk, exactly the way Rebecca had marked them.

"That's mine on the left, Jack," he said. "The other is something written by Timothy Morton in the late seventies. It was in a magazine."

Jack Hart, a *Post* foreign correspondent and White House reporter before coming to the editorial page, was a man who was moderate in just about everything, from his early forties age, height, and weight to his shirt size and his opinions. Even his office on the seventh floor of the *Post* building on 15th Street Northwest was moderately sized—and decorated with framed copies of front pages of the *Post* and watercolors of flowers. He and R had first met a couple of years ago at a Library of Congress symposium on journalism as history.

Jack immediately noticed the bright red underlines on each of the articles. Silently, he read the ones on his left—R's piece—and then on Morton's.

Back and forth his head went, a second and then a third time.

"So what's the urgent problem?" he said to R.

"Maybe I should have made it clearer that some of the points were patterned after what Morton had written," said R.

"You did." Jack lifted the op-ed piece and read out loud: " 'Timothy Morton, in a most perceptive essay in 1977, had proclaimed the need for Benjamin Franklin to be given his rightful place in our hearts and minds—as well as our history books.' All you did from then on is relate, through paraphrasing mostly, what he wished for to what has finally happened."

"Some of the wording later could be too similar."

"All right," said Jack, beginning to read again. "You said for instance, that Franklin had always been known for flying kites and making up platitudes—more or less. So did Morton. So what? I don't get the problem. You didn't steal any direct quotes. Had you just read Morton's piece before writing yours?"

R nodded.

"That happens a lot. You read something, put it aside and write your own, and some of the other guy's stuff sticks. It's no big deal."

R shook his head.

"Somebody's about to try to make it a big deal?"

"I'm afraid so."

Jack put the two clippings one on top of the other and handed them back across his desk. "What's gotten into you historian types of late? Everybody seems to be running either scared or at each other."

"Well said, Jack."

"What do you want me to do about this?"

"Will you publish a letter of amplification—something like this?" R put a piece of white copy paper on the desk. On it he had written:

There was an inadvertent omission of full attribution in my recent op-ed piece on Benjamin Franklin. While there was a mention of an earlier essay by Timothy Morton, there could have been other, more specific attribution given to some of the Morton material.

I very much regret the omission—and I apologize to Mr. Morton.

R. Raymond Taylor

Jack read it. "Following the old maxim, 'The best defense is a good offense,' " he said. "Is that it?"

"That's it."

"I don't think it's necessary—but whatever pleases you, pleases me. I have something to show you too, by the way."

Jack shoved a manila folder toward him. There were five, maybe six, opened letters in it.

"Our loyal readers have risen up," said Jack, "to point out that while there is no *major* memorial to Ben Franklin in D.C., there is, in fact, a marvelous statue of the man in front of the old post office building on Pennsylvania Avenue."

R had seen the statue a number of times, but it was not the same as a monument on the Mall, which had been his point. He skimmed through the letters. One gave some of the statue's history—sculpted in marble by Jacques Jouvenal, dedicated on Ben's birthday, January 17, 1889, by Ben's granddaughter Mrs. H. W. Emory....

"It turns out the statue was a gift from Stilson Hutchins, the founder of this newspaper," said Jack.

"If you want to include a line about it in my little note, feel free to do so."

"Great idea—done."

R heaped thanks on Jack Hart and caught the elevator back downstairs, where he hailed a taxi. He considered having the driver go over to Pennsylvania Avenue to look at the Ben statue again but he decided to go directly to Union Station to get on with his day. He arrived in time to catch the 11 A.M. Acela express to Philadelphia.

A bush bearing gifts was waiting for him at 30th Street Station some ninety minutes later.

. . .

"Welcome to Philadelphia, the City of Brotherly Love," said Harry Dickinson. "I thought you'd never get here."

"How in hell did you know I'd be on this train?" said a most unhappy R. He knew his voice was too loud, but he didn't care. *Leave me alone, Harry Dickinson!*

"I didn't. This is the third train from Washington I've met. I just came down from New York this morning to see you. I haven't left the train station. Your girl told me you were coming—"

"She's not my girl!" yelled R. "She's a professional historian—a Ph.D., a scholar! She works for Benjamin Franklin University!"

Harry, bushy as ever, put up his hands as if to say, Shush, please. "OK, OK, I'm sorry. Pipe down. They'll have the cops on us in a moment."

R looked around. People were indeed staring at him. Here in this marvelous high-ceiling cavern of a train station, there were travelers who had stopped to see what the man in the tweed jacket and blue button-down shirt was ranting about. Was he a terrorist? Was he crazy? Why would anybody scream in 30th Street Station? Isn't this exciting? Or is it scary?

R rolled his eyes and waved at a couple of the spectators. They began moving again, away from the obviously mentally deranged man.

"Come with me upstairs to the Amtrak Cub so we can talk," Harry said. "I bring tidings—tidings of great joy, to coin a phrase."

R angrily shook himself away from Harry and took a step toward the door where the taxis lined up. "I don't want to hear your tidings."

"Come with me or I'll throw a fit and shout, even louder than you. I'll claim you made a pass at me. They'll have a Sex Crimes SWAT team in here in a blink, and away we'll both go to jail—"

"All right, all right. Five minutes, that's it," said R. "Five minutes of tidings and I'm gone."

He followed Harry up a flight of stairs on the north side of the lobby, behind and to the right of the ticket windows. There Harry pushed a button, a glass door buzzed open, and they were admitted to a private waiting area for first class and other privileged passengers. An attendant at a desk verified that Harry rated the privilege. The place was quiet and private, with some comfortable chairs and couches, hot coffee and cold drinks, and a few things to read.

Harry led R to the rear of the long narrow club room to a

soundproof conference room that, according to a small sign, was UNOCCUPIED.

They went inside and closed the door.

"The five-minute clock is running," said R, sitting down at a six-chair conference table across from Harry.

"I have in my pocket two pieces of paper. One is a check, the other is a contract," Harry began. "The check is for half a million dollars, the contract is for a book to be delivered within a year—working title *Ben Three.*"

R closed his eyes and tried to digest what he had just heard. Half a million dollars? Did this idiot just say he had a check in his pocket for half a million dollars?

"A second half million will be paid to you upon final delivery of, and sign-off on, a satisfactory manuscript. In other words, the advance is one million dollars. That puts you up there in the bestseller league of the book-writing world, Dr. R. Raymond Taylor."

One million dollars. The idiot said one million dollars. Let's see, at the level of life I'm now living, thought R, that should last me until the age of eighty—with a lot left over for the kids. Kids? There are no kids. Samantha, do you want to have some kids? Maybe we should talk about that. How old are you, by the way? Isn't it interesting that I don't know?

"No, thanks," said R. He made a motion to stand.

"You promised me five minutes. I would argue that you are not selling out Wally at all. For God's sake, R, if you wrote *Ben Two,* that means awarding the Pulitzer Prize to Wally was an act of deceit—"

"If that's the case, then, goddamn you, Harry, you're as guilty of the deceit as anyone else!"

Harry glanced away, but only for a second. "Damn me all you wish. The fact is, Wally would want it corrected."

"That is the purest of a pure lie, and you know it. If he had something he wanted corrected he would have done so while he was still alive—or even after his death—in some kind of written statement. Maybe even in his will."

Harry was smiling.

"What's your problem?" R said, his manner still most hostile.

"I think you just confirmed that you wrote *Ben Two.*"

Until recently, R had not been a violence-prone person. He had never raised a hand or a fist to anybody in his life; not even when he was a kid did he get into fights. His quarterback skills at high school football centered not on brawn or aggressiveness but on his throwing arm, agility, and brains.

But here he was again, as he had been with Rebecca a few days ago at Elbow's party, aching to beat the last breath out of somebody—this time, Harry Dickinson.

Harry must have sensed something along that line. He lowered his voice and said, "Look, R, I understand your emotions on this. Wally was a friend of mine too. He lived a lie and, yes, I helped him live it. But you not only have a right to expose the lie, you have a responsibility to the public and to your profession."

R was calming down a bit. Harry's life was no longer in danger.

"You're a man of history, R. You have dedicated your life to the pursuit of the truth. How in hell can you stand by—stand back, really—and let a falsehood of authorship and accomplishment continue?"

R stood up.

"What if I blow the whistle on you anyhow?" Harry said. "What if I say publicly that *Ben Two,* a book I edited, was published and praised and honored under false pretenses? What if I tell the world that Wally Rush, a good and honorable man, did not in fact write *Ben Two,* and I believe the real author was none other than his longtime assistant, R Taylor?"

Harry stood and removed two items from an inside breast pocket of the dark blue blazer he was wearing. He laid them out on the table between them.

R didn't want to glance down but he simply could not stop himself.

There was a light green Green Tree Publishers check for $500,000, made payable to R. Raymond Taylor. The other item was a sheath of legal-size papers, AUTHOR CONTRACT at the top of the first page.

R looked but did not touch. "Harry, this is the end of our discussion. Without my confirmation you have nothing. There is no one else who knows anything about what happened with *Ben Two*. All I will say to you now is that it is not—was not—as simple, as black and white, as you believe."

R had spoken softly. The steam was gone from the exchange—from him.

Harry put the check and the contract back in his pocket. R probably imagined it, but he seemed wilted.

"My early presidency book is still available if you'd like to make an offer," R said, at the door to the conference room.

"I'll take a pass, but thanks," said Harry.

"Why *did* you go ahead and publish that book under Wally's name?"

"It was a superbly written, well-researched book that was clearly going to be a critical and a popular success. That's my business. I publish such books."

"Even if Wally didn't write it—or so you suspected?"

"I figured what I only suspected—but didn't know for sure—wouldn't hurt me."

"Do you realize that in most other businesses you could go to jail for what you did?"

Harry laughed out loud at the absurdity of such a thing happening in *his* business.

. . .

"Surprise!"

When Clara Hopkins said this playfully to R the second he stepped inside Gray House, he almost yelled again. The last thing in the world he wanted right now was another surprise. His reaction was annoyance and more—anger.

But he held his tongue and followed her into Wally's old study. A standing easel there was covered by a large piece of white cloth that had the appearance of a bedsheet.

"Here goes," she said, whisking the cloth away in the ta-da! manner of a TV quiz show prize unveiling.

There, fully exposed on the easel, was a large piece of heavy posterboard with small portraits across the top. Under each was a column of words and numbers; at the very top in heavy black writing was SEPTEMBER 7, 1788.

"Ask and you shall receive," said Clara. R noticed she was still as gorgeous as ever—maybe even more so. She was dressed today in a tailored dark brown suit that showed off her hair, complexion, and eyes....

She's a professional historian, a Ph.D., a scholar! R shifted his concentration to what was on the easel.

Across the top there were five-by-seven pictures of Ben, Adams, Hamilton, Madison, and Washington. Underneath was a chronology for each man for that day in large black block letters.

"Do you want me to run through it for you?" said Clara. She was clearly proud of her work.

"Please ... yes, that would be great," said R, clearly impressed by her work.

Clara grabbed a two-foot-long silver pointer. She placed the tip on Ben's portrait, which was a black and white copy of the so-called fur-collar painting done in Paris by Joseph Siffred Duplessis in 1778. Ben liked it so much he refused ever to pose for another, telling all other pleading artists simply to copy the Duplessis.

"Let's begin with our man. He was already very sick then, as you know. Gout, stomach pain, intestinal infections—who knows what-all was hurting."

She moved the pointer down the information below Ben's picture.

"— Awoke in Market Street home in Philadelphia.
— Lunched at home.
— Spent afternoon in bed.
— Doctor visited before dark.
— Ate dinner in bed."

Clara said, in summary, "Ben never left the house all day."

"How sure are you of that?"

"Ninety-five percent."

"Why not one hundred?"

"I'm not one hundred percent sure of my own name."

R smiled. This woman really was a professional.

She moved the pointer to John Adams. He was scowling, per usual.

With her pointer, she went through his day:

"— In Quincy, at home until late morning.
— Had lunch in Boston with old friend Thaddeus Wilson.
— Returned to Quincy, spent afternoon writing letters.
— Ate early dinner, was in bed, presumably asleep, by dark."

"A typical day for old John, in other words," said R, trying to hide his delight at what the pattern was so far. "Did he growl at anybody, profess his righteousness to anyone?"

"The record is silent on that," said Clara, "but one can only assume that it was a day like any other day and he did one or the other—or both."

Alexander Hamilton was next. His usual expression said loud and clear that he was intellectually superior to all humans, most particularly on matters concerning finance and commerce. R believed Hamilton to be right about that. None of the other Founding Fathers, including Ben, were in Hamilton's league on economics. Jefferson and Madison operated their own farm operations in the red. Some scholars claimed Washington had to marry rich to keep a roof over his head. Ben made a lot of money and was a terrific businessman, but his knowledge of high finance was never on the scale of Hamilton's. Samantha would have been much wiser to have chosen Hamilton rather than Hancock. R himself briefly considered once trying to do the once-and-for-all book on the duel with Aaron Burr that cost Hamilton his life. Someday, maybe after the early presidency book, he might do it yet.

Clara went through Hamilton's September 7, 1788:

"— In New York City, at his house on Fifth Avenue.
— Met all day, or much of the day, with various legal clients.
— No word on lunch or dinner.
— No record on evening activities."

"So he could have left the city?"

"Yes, but not for long. He was definitely at a meeting the next morning—on the eighth—with several bankers downtown. There are written accounts of the meeting. The discussion was about creating a central federal bank."

On to James Madison. There was very little written under his photograph.

Clara said, "He was a most meticulous man, as you know, R. but for some reason there's not much about his activities that day. The people who tend to his papers in Charlottesville think it's most likely he was in Montpelier, at least for part of the day. But they—I—need more time to fill out the rest. The records must be somewhere. We just haven't found them yet. I will pursue it further."

R had always believed that Madison, the tiny man with the giant brain, had been shortchanged by the American Revolution historian community. Maybe, like Ben, his time would eventually come.

They moved their attention to George Washington. There was a long list of items below his picture, which was a copy-machine replica of the famous Gilbert Stuart portrait.

"— Spent the night before at Leesburg, Virginia, having ridden there by horseback from Mount Vernon.
— Rode on west, crossed Shenandoah River at Harpers Ferry, proceeded to Charles Town.
— Dined as a guest of James Nourse at his home, Piedmont.
— Spent night two miles down the road at home of brother, Samuel Washington."

She turned to face R, the pointer held in front of her like an at-ease baton. "End of presentation, sir."

R clapped his hands. Clara bowed, accepting the applause.

"This really is an impressive performance, Clara," R said. "Thank you very much."

"Now will you say why you asked me to do this?" she said. "Will you please, *please,* tell me what's going on?"

"Sorry, I can't do that."

"Why not?"

He shrugged. "I'm going over to Clymer's office now."

"Do you want me to call first, to make sure Elbow's there? I heard . . . somewhere . . . that he may have had travel plans for the day."

"I'll chance it. Thanks."

And he was out the door.

Yes, R wanted to talk to Elbow Clymer. But, more important, he wanted time to consider the message of Clara's little easel-board presentation.

There could not possibly have been a meeting of Ben, Adams, Hamilton, Madison, and Washington on September 7, 1788!

So. The whole thing was a hoax, like the Prophecy? Those papers were manufactured and then stuck in the lining of that old cloak to be found someday?

But who would do something like that? And why?

Questions. Oh, yes, there were many natural follow-up questions. But what mattered right now was that there had been no Founding Fathers jury of peers gathering on September 7, 1788.

Hooray! Hooray for Ben! Hooray for Wally!

TWELVE

Gray House was five blocks from the BFU administration building where Clymer's office was located. R had walked only three of those blocks, barely inside the campus, before he stopped and sat down at Deborah Read Franklin Park, the only place on earth named for Ben's terribly treated and neglected wife. It was a small place with a couple of beds of roses and a few stone benches.

Even Wally never made an effort to defend the atrocious way Ben treated Deborah. "Like an ugly unwanted stray dog," was the way Wally once put it. The only thing Ben did for her was agree to take her as his common-law wife after her legal husband, a low-life crook, ran off to the Caribbean to avoid the law. She bore Ben two children, one of whom died in childhood, and stayed in Philadelphia while Ben was living high and well in London and later in Paris. When told that Deborah was dying, Ben didn't even rouse himself to get on a boat to go home. Wally used to say their letters had all the warmth, feeling, and passion of credit rating reports. If Ben's conduct toward her bothered him very much he kept such confessions to himself. Maybe Clara was right to see if there was a way to finally give the poor woman her due....

R took out his cell phone and called Wes Braxton in Eastville.

"I have a buyer for the papers, Wes," he said. "Are you in a position to sell?"

"The Ross family has said it's fine with them," said Wes. "We have twelve members on our board, and I've talked to all but two of them. So far, it's fine."

"Good . . . that's good."

"What kind of price is your buyer talking about?"

R. took a breath—a thought—and said, "Even more than I expected. Twenty-one thousand dollars."

"Oh, my God!" Wes Braxton was almost squealing. "That'll do it—it's a deal! I know the other two board people will go along."

R said that was terrific, and they both added a few more words of mutual congratulation.

Then Wes asked, "Who is the buyer, if I may ask?"

"As a matter of fact, he wants to remain anonymous," said R. "He will pay me, and I will send you my personal check for twenty-one thousand. OK?"

"Great. This may do it."

"Do what?"

"Get me the director's job—or put me on the search list at the very least. It proves I can raise money too."

R said he was glad to be of help.

Then he walked on to the administration building and upstairs to the second-floor office of Elbridge Clymer. The time had come to deal with the BFU offer.

But Clara was right once again. Elbow was gone—out of town for the day. His secretary, a woman in her fifties, expected R, however.

"President Clymer said you might be coming by, Dr. Taylor. He said if you did I should give you this."

She handed him a sealed white envelope. There was a large *R* in blue on the front, *Confidential* down in the left-hand corner.

R took it back outside to his bench and opened it.

R:

Clara told me you might be coming up today. I feel terrible about what I have to tell you—and about having to do it in a letter—but I'm not going to be able to pull off the Wally institute deal after all. I am sick about it because of what I said to you. In the wake and emotion of Wally's death, I simply spoke too soon. It turns out that I was on the short list for the presidency of another quite major university. I had no idea I was going to get the job, so I continued going about my business at BFU with the assumption that I was not. That is why I spoke to you about the new Franklin research institute possibility. Well, I have been offered the other presidency. It is a position I simply cannot refuse; I am sure you will agree when it becomes public in the next few days. The formal offer came just yesterday. It means I will be leaving BFU and thus will be unable to provide resources needed to create the Franklin study institute. I am so sorry.

I look forward to speaking to you in more detail about this in person.

And—who knows—an opportunity for something similar for you could in fact develop at my new university home. Clara has agreed to keep Wally's ship afloat on an interim basis here until all matters shake down. She has turned out to be quite a find.

My best,
Elbow.

R folded the letter, returned it to the envelope, and went off in search of a taxi to take him back to 30th Street Station.

. . .

Once again, R went to the Quiet Car, which was just behind the engine on this particular Metroliner. He had no desire to talk on his cell phone or listen while anyone else talked on theirs. As a courtesy, he had called Clara from the taxi to tell her he was returning to Washington. She didn't seem surprised.

Obviously she and Clymer were in a high state of—to use Elbow's word—finding each other.

The Quiet Car was barely half full. R found a double seat all to himself, planning to sit silently by the window, meditatively watching the Eastern Corridor world of Pennsylvania, Delaware, and Maryland pass by.

The train began moving.

He felt the presence of a person in the aisle by his seat. The conductor, an attendant . . .

It was Harry Dickinson!

"I know we can't talk here," Harry whispered. "Come with me back to the Café Car."

R moved his head to the left, to the right, to the left, to the right. If head movements could kill, Harry Dickinson, famous editor, would have been a dead man.

"Seriously, R. We have a crisis." Harry's face, at least the part R could see, did have an uncharacteristically grim look.

He had no choice. So he went with Harry through a regular Business Class chair car to the Café Car, which was also not crowded. They sat down across a brown Formica-topped table.

"First, I want to know how you knew I was on this train," R said.

"I saw you go downstairs to the track," said Harry. "I didn't tell you I planned to join you because you might have caused another scene."

He had that right, thought R. There was no telling what kind of reaction just the sight of this world-famous editor might have triggered.

"Clara, the ashes woman—that Ph.D. scholar, superb serious human being, whatever—told me just a few minutes ago when I called that you were on your way to catch a train."

R remembered a recent movie where two guys threw one of their mothers off a speeding train—or tried to.

Harry moved on to the crisis.

"After we talked there at Thirtieth Street Station, I stayed in the lounge and made some telephone calls to my office and elsewhere while waiting for the next Acela back to New York. Rebecca Kendall Lee has declared war, R. That's the crisis."

R held up his right hand. "I have taken care of the problem. There will be a little something in *The Washington Post* in the morning. I've headed her off. She can't touch me."

"It's not you, R. It's one of the other committee members."

"Sonya Lyman said she'll be fine, too. We can survive Rebecca. What Rebecca did was pure unambiguous plagiarism. Neither Sonya nor I are guilty of anything even remotely similar."

Harry was looking off to the right. All there was to see were the oil refineries and storage tanks along the Delaware River.

"It's not her either, R. It's John Gwinnett."

R couldn't believe he heard right. *John Gwinnett!*

Harry went on quickly, excitedly. "I'm John's editor. We have been working on his Patrick Henry opus for eleven years. The book is nearly eight hundred pages long, including graphics and footnotes, a masterpiece of research, the crowning achievement of a distinguished career. It's set for publication next year, at the top of our fall nonfiction list. First printing probably a quarter of a million, who knows. What I can tell you, R, is that it really is a terrific book. Every detail of Patrick Henry's life is there. It's a fascinating story, one that's going to awaken interest in Henry like nothing ever has before. John got access to every scrap of paper most everybody in the world has, pertaining to Henry, and wrote it beautifully. He didn't really need me much, to tell you the truth. Some of his descriptions of life in Virginia, particularly during those critical days in Williamsburg, would make a Tory-lover cry."

Were those tears in Harry's own eyes? Yes. *I didn't know he had tears in him!*

R said, "Coffee or something, Harry?"

"Great, yes. A glass of white wine. Thanks, R."

R walked to the center of the car to the service counter and returned in a few minutes with two small twist-cap bottles of white wine and two plastic glasses.

In silence, each fixed his own drink and took a couple of long swallows. The train was now in the familiar northern outskirts of Wilmington.

"Rebecca Lee called me. She said she found an article John wrote thirty-seven years ago for a small historical review published in Georgia by Emory University. The subject was how the introduction of tobacco changed life forever in the South. There were some sentences in it that Rebecca matched to a Ph.D. thesis written by a University of North Carolina professor twelve years earlier. Rebecca says if John's ARHA committee takes any public action against her, she will spill the beans on John."

There was the derelict bus again. The train was nearing the Wilmington station.

"How many sentences are involved?" R asked.

"Three."

"How close are the matches?"

"Identical—almost."

"How almost?"

"All but a couple of words are the same."

R just shook his head. He couldn't believe this. Not John Gwinnett.

"I know, I know," Harry said. "There's no excuse."

"If they just weren't identical. Nobody accidentally uses somebody else's sentences exactly. It's impossible. You know that as well as I do. Paraphrasing can be done innocently. That's what she claims she caught me doing. But not identical sentences."

"I know, I know."

The train came to a halt at Wilmington station.

R said, after it started moving again, "What's on the table—you know, if anything—as to what to do about this?" R couldn't believe he had just used the phrase *you know*! First it was cop talk; now he was reverting to high school jock talk.

Harry lowered his head. R read this as a sure signal that Harry was not proud of what he was about to say. "Your committee—John's committee—issues a statement that says something . . . I don't know . . . that the evidence about Rebecca Kendall Lee is inconclusive and that further research and investigation needs to be done. Then it's forgotten in the course of time."

"Did John Gwinnett ask you to talk to me about this?"

"No, no. God, no. All he did when I passed on Rebecca's threat was laugh."

"Laugh? He sees the prospect of being accused of plagiarism funny? Is he all right?"

Harry just shook his head. "Do you think Sonya Lyman could be persuaded to back off for a while?"

"Probably," said R. *Definitely,* he thought.

"I'm not his editor—but we publish Joe Hooper's stuff."

Harry looked back out the window and so did R. Neither wanted to have eye contact with the other on the real meaning of what Harry had just implied. If it became necessary, Green Tree Press had the means to get Hooper to go along, although based on his statement about not lynching Rebecca, it would probably not be a major problem.

Soon the train was on the long bridge over the water of the Susquehanna River where it flows into Chesapeake Bay. Baltimore was not far away.

"Three little sentences, thirty-seven long years ago, R," Harry said. "With the exception of murder and treason, most other crimes have statutes of limitations."

"Fine, but what you're suggesting is giving in to the crime of blackmail by Rebecca Lee *now*," R said. "She'll get away with really blatant plagiarism scot-free."

"Maybe it's a worthy trade-off. Otherwise, for three sentences she'll ruin John's reputation, his legacy, his life, his everything—never mind the Patrick Henry book."

"She wouldn't be the one who did that, Harry. *He* did it to himself—if that's what finally happens. Just like she did it to *herself* in that awful Reagan book."

"Forget her. Think of John. Thirty-seven years. Three sentences. Think about what you're saying, R. A good man commits plagiarism in the heat of youth, and you will permit this vicious woman to ruin his life thirty-seven years later? Clearly, he hasn't even come close to doing anything like that again or she would have found it."

A conductor came through the car. "Baltimore. Next stop Baltimore."

R welcomed the interruption. His mind was racing. He needed no more turn-on words from Harry Dickinson.

Then, several seconds later, came a male-voiced public address announcement that said Baltimore was now only three minutes away. "Please watch your step when exiting the train. There is a space between the train and the platform. . . ."

"What's your verdict?" Harry asked.

"I've got five days. That's when, according to an e-mail I got yesterday, we'll have our big confrontation with Rebecca in Williamsburg."

"Fine." Harry stood up.

"Where you going?" R asked.

"I'll get off here in Baltimore and catch the next train back to New York. Thanks, R. One more thing."

R could do without one more thing from Harry Dickinson.

"Rebecca Lee also dropped a line about how she always suspected that somebody other than Wally wrote *Ben Two. Maybe R Taylor?* That's a direct quote. She reminded me that she was still a member in good standing of the Ben Crowd at the time. She said she might have some expert do a style comparison between *Ben Two* and your writing. I told her to be my guest."

"You *what?*"

"Relax, R. She's bluffing. I'm the only one who is expert enough to prove anything like that, and obviously I'm not available. Only three people knew the secret. one of them, Wally, is dead and that leaves only you and me."

Before R could throw out Ben's line about secrets between two people, the Bush was gone.

R was struck by the fact that Harry Dickinson, famous editor of famous books, had spent most of this particular workday in the vineyards of American literature riding trains up and down the Northeast Corridor.

He finished his wine and returned to the Quiet Car to curse Rebecca Lee in silence and recall and consider what Ben had said to him in London about choices.

.   .   .

There was a voice mail at home from Samantha, maybe the happiest and best she had ever left him at any time in their five years together.

Oh, R, it's finally happening. I've got Mr. Hancock right
where I want him. I get him and he gets me. We talked
for hours last night. He's not a jerk after all. The words
are flowing. So are the ideas. I never ever thought it
would happen but it is, it is, it is! I feel like David Mc-
Cullough must have felt when he was really into John
Adams. I'll bet he talked to Adams. Didn't you say you
thought he did? I feel the way Wally must have when he
was writing *Ben One*—and *Ben Two*.

I love you.

Oh, dear Samantha. If you only knew what the man you say you
love has been doing the last few days: talking to Ben's naked ghost
in the parlor at 36 Craven Street, turning down a million dollars,
considering going along with a blackmail threat from a young plagiarist to protect an old plagiarist. . . .

Oh, my God, if you only knew that Ben had said all Hancock
deserves is an aphorism.

And if you only knew what the man you say you love—me—is
going to do right now.

R went to his desk in the study, unlocked the top right drawer,
and removed his checkbook. On a blank check, he put the date
and made the check out to *The Eastern Pennsylvania Museum of
Early Colonial History;* wrote after A M O U N T, *Twenty-one thousand dollars;* and, on the F O R line, *Eighteenth-century papers.* He
signed the check, placed it in an envelope, and addressed it to Wes
Braxton at the museum in Eastville.

It was only after he had sealed the envelope that he realized he
had forgotten to include a note of some kind. Something handwritten and as brief as *Thanks, yours in Early American History,
R,* would have been enough. He considered tearing it open and
doing everything again except the check but decided against it.

The money—less than a third of what he had in his savings and checking accounts together—was enough of a thank-you. The important thing was that the sealed envelope meant that the twelve pieces of paper from the cloak were now his. They belonged to him. They were his property. He could do with them whatever he pleased.

Now for the very last to-do.

From a small briefcase he had kept locked in another desk drawer, he removed those twelve pieces of paper as well as his written summary of the stories they seemed to tell.

He laid them all out in front of him on the desk as he had that first day at Eastville and again at Wally's. He wanted to look at them one more time.

R had never been much for ceremony and ritual, but he was suddenly overcome with a desire to perform this with some panache—something that fit the specialness of the occasion.

Only one way came to mind.

He went into the kitchen and came back with a box of long wooden matches. Then he took the papers and the matches to the empty fireplace in the living room. As a tiny little effect, he went back to the library for an eight-by-ten framed print of David Martin's famous 1766 *Renaissance Man* portrait of Ben. Dressed elegantly in a velvet coat and a powdered wig, his silver-rimmed glasses down on his nose, he is sitting in a gilded chair at a table, his right thumb under his chin, reading some papers. A white marble bust of Isaac Newton is off to the right.

Now all was ready. . . .

No. One more thing. R went back to the study for a copy of *Ben Two,* the advance one Wally had signed and given to him—with a wink—fresh from the publisher long before official publication. Wally's inscription was:

To R—
I really couldn't have done it without you.
   Wally

R placed the book on the mantel too, after resisting the temptation to possibly involve it in this ceremony in a more significant way. . . .

One by one, he set afire and dropped into the fireplace each of the twelve pages of what may—or may not—have been Joshiah Ross's notes of a historical meeting about horrendous crime and nonpunishment involving the Founding Fathers of the United States of America.

He was careful to make sure each sheet of paper was fully burned before lighting another match and doing the next.

Maybe he should have put on some music. But what? "America"? "For He's a Wally Good Fellow"? "Seventy-six Trombones"?

Maybe he should have said something, raised a glass of calvados in a toast. And said what? Maybe something like, *To Ben, may the celebration of the tricentennial of your birth be great! And free of phony hoax-driven controversy about murders!*

R's own notes were the last to disappear into flames.

Once it was gone, R used a heavy brass poker to spread the ashes around on the bottom of the fireplace until they were, like Wally, only dust.

Now it was impossible to tell what they had once been or to ever put them back together so what was written on them could be read.

R felt good about what he had just done. As a professional historian, he had made a decision—yes, a choice of Honor—to prevent the unwarranted smearing of Benjamin Franklin, our First American.

Yes, Ben fathered an illegitimate child named William. The

whole world knew that. But, no, that son did not come from Ben's having impregnated a child, possibly as young as twelve.

And, no matter any of his other possible sins, he certainly didn't commission someone to have William's mother stabbed to death and her bloody body stuffed in a gunnysack and tossed into the Delaware River.

R was sure of it.

THIRTEEN

Then, late morning four days later, Clara called from Philadelphia.

"I have more on that day in 1788," she announced with an urgent and pleased rush in her voice.

R took a very deep breath.

"Remember what I said about James Madison, that I hadn't been able to come up with anything about where or what Madison was doing that day?"

R mumbled something to acknowledge that he did remember.

"Well, my friend at the Madison Papers archives at U-Va called me back. She said a huge mystery had arisen as a result of my original inquiry. She said Madison kept daily precise notes about everything he did. But get this."

R felt a sudden certainty that he did not want to get this.

"His notes from September seventh of that year and from the days before and after—September sixth and eighth—are missing. My friend said it was possible they somehow were misplaced through the years but—and I quote—'It's also possible somebody,

Madison himself even, intentionally destroyed them. Who knows?' End quote. That got me to wondering."

R was breathing again but only barely. A touch of nausea was forming somewhere down near the bottom of his throat.

Clara continued. "I went back through each of the rundowns I had on the other Founding Fathers and did some more work with each of their papers—through various Web sites and CD-ROMs as well as colleagues. Guess what?"

R declined to guess.

"First, it turns out that the big bank meeting Hamilton supposedly attended in New York on September eighth was actually a week later. His archivists at Columbia now have some second thoughts about where he was on the seventh and eighth. He may not have been in New York after all, and maybe somebody played with the diary entries. They're going to get back to me once they sort it out.

"Second, Martha Washington, in a letter to her sister dated two weeks after September seventh, said, and I quote: 'George travels away from Mount Vernon much, much too much to suit me, and, I fear, his health. He still labors for his country. He departed on a trip several days ago in the middle of the night, would not tell me his destination, and upon his return asked that I forever keep secret his absence. I can only assume he was doing work on behalf of our new and great nation. Bless his heart and his soul.'

"Third, Franklin was seen at a friend's house in Philadelphia the evening of September sixth, so he was definitely not confined to his bed during that whole week, as a notebook from his doctor had said. The doctor, as I'm sure you know, was a close friend of Franklin's and would not be resistant to requests from Franklin to change something. There is good solid evidence that the doctor often covered for him on a number of other earlier occasions for numerous other reasons, including those of a different kind of bed."

Yes, but that hardly proved anything, thought R, grateful for even a tiny opening for a possible challenge to what was clearly developing. Ben was Ben. . . .

"Fourth, the Adams papers at the Massachusetts Historical Society show a direct conflict between the records of John and Abigail. She said John was 'away from us and our hearth' on September sixth, seventh, and eighth, while John, in a letter that appears to experts from the shakiness of the handwriting to have been written later, talks of 'good talk and food among family and friends' those days in Quincy. Most important, there are a few lines that turned up in another letter that Adams wrote to Madison in late September of 1788. Shall I read them?"

R grunted a reluctant affirmative.

" 'It was most wise of you to suggest that we leave no carriage tracks, so to speak, no lingering odors from our recent gathering. I have seen to it. I trust that our colleagues have done the same.' "

Oh, my God. R remembered Johnny Rutledge talking years ago about a reference to Ben's saying something about Madison and a "difficult situation." R had put it out of his mind until now— or, most precisely, until it popped out while he was sitting on the parlor floor at 36 Craven Street several days ago.

"It's all adding up, isn't it?" said Clara.

R made a sound. He was sick to his stomach. He thought he might throw up. He thought he might faint. He thought he might die.

He knew he had to lie to Clara.

"Good work," he said, trying his best to sound sincere, serious, strong. "Thank you."

"Thank *you.* Now will you tell me? Now will you tell me why September 7, 1788, is so important?

"I can't do that."

"What were they covering up, if that's what this is all about? Is that it, our nation's first Watergate cover-up?"

"All I can say is what I said a moment ago, Clara. Thank you. Now I have to go."

"What's going on? Go where?"

To my destruction as a historian and as a person of honor and purpose!

"To the bathroom," he said.

It was almost the truth. R hung up the telephone, put his head on his desk, closed his eyes, and experienced the opening thoughts and scenes of a nightmare that, he was certain, would be with him, and in him, for the rest of his life. . . .

Eventually, he rose from his desk, but instead of going to the bathroom, he went to the front room, to the fireplace where, just a few evenings ago, he had turned to ashes those twelve sheets of paper from the Eastville cloak.

He so wanted to look down and find that, through some miracle, the ashes had re-formed into what they had been: a coded account of what very well may have been a most historic meeting of Founding Fathers at a Pennsylvania farmhouse more than two hundred years ago.

No such miracle had occurred.

. . .

There he was. And there was Ben, standing eight feet tall in dirty white marble atop a pedestal that was nearly ten feet high itself.

The statue here at Twelfth and Pennsylvania Avenue really was stunning. The *Post* letter-to-the-editor writers were probably correct in complaining that R should have at least mentioned it in his op-ed piece.

Ben was wearing an open long diplomatic coat with huge buttons and fur collar, a waistcoat, a frilly tied neckpiece, and matching fluffy shirt cuffs coming out the end of the coat sleeves, tight breeches to the knee, with stockings over the legs down to his shoes. His build was solid except in the middle, where his potbelly pooched out, the buttons on the waistcoat clearly straining to keep it contained. His bald forehead gave way to long hair dropping over his ears and—when viewed from the rear—down his back. He was not wearing glasses.

His right hand and forearm were raised; his mouth was closed. There was a book in his left hand down by his side. Three more books, one open, the other two closed, were stacked behind his right foot. His legs were apart, his right slightly ahead of the left.

His face was animated, pleasant. He was busy. Was he about to speak?

FRANKLIN was written at the top of the gray granite pedestal in six-inch raised letters. The sculptor's name was engraved above that, underneath Ben's left foot. Below were four words in the granite, one on each side: PATRIOT, PHILOSOPHER, PHILAN-THROPIST, PRINTER. Farther down the base was a brass plaque that said the statue was erected on January 17, 1889.

The statue and the pedestal sat in the center of a round step-up slab, one foot high and twenty feet in diameter, that was made of concrete and brick.

R recognized this man on the pedestal. It was Benjamin Franklin, all right. And, it occurred to him, this statue could probably also pass for Wally Rush if it were on its back in an open casket.

From a nearby plaque, R read that the statue had originally been at Tenth and Pennsylvania in front of what was then the *Washington Post* building after it was "Presented to the National Capitol" by the *Post*'s publisher. It was moved here in the 1980s to adorn the entrance to the towered structure that was once the headquarters for the U.S. Post Office Department. It was still owned by the government but was now called the Old Post Office Pavilion and was mostly leased out to small tourist shops and cafés downstairs, with various government agency offices on the floors above.

The post office–Ben angle certainly made sense. As deputy postmaster general for the pre-Revolution colonies under the King, Ben launched the first real mail service in America. And that was just one item of hundreds on the extremely long list of this remarkable man's achievements.

The thought reaffirmed to R the correctness of his original impulse to turn those Eastville papers into ashes. This man, this incredible human being and Founding Father, flawed though he may have been, did not deserve to have his reputation smeared now over some accusations that appeared to be part of a hoax.

But...

Probable hoax or not, I am a historian, a pursuer and teller of the truth.

But...

Probable hoax or not, how dare I play God with those twelve sheets of history?

But...

Probable hoax or not, wouldn't it have been more professional, more ethical, more everything to have simply locked them up someplace rather than destroy them?

But...

Probable hoax or not, what would I have done if they told terrible tales about Adams? Or Jefferson? Or even Washington?

But. But. But.

It's done. The papers are no more. Forget it.

. . .

After the message from Clara, he had rushed outside and started walking. He went down to M Street and kept going east, taking the fork onto Pennsylvania, until forty-five minutes later he was here, looking up at Ben.

R figured it was one thing to speak with Ben the Naked Ghost across a London parlor; it was quite another to chat with Ben the

Statue amid the heavy pedestrian traffic along Pennsylvania Avenue.

R slowly walked once around the statue. Then a second and a third time. He stared at Ben from the front for a good two minutes and then from the rear. Then from one side and the other. This angle and that angle.

The statue needed a good cleaning. There were signs of gross marble deterioration in several spots, particularly up on the back of Ben's coat. R made annoyed note of that. But he had no idea what he was really looking for, even what he was doing here. Was he hoping for inspiration? Wisdom? Affirmation?

You did the right thing, young man. I thank you for your choice of Honor.

Maybe that's what R wanted to imagine he heard from Ben.

If so, it hadn't happened.

There were people all around the statue, walking in and out of the building, up and down the street. Some were tourists, others workers from the various federal office buildings in the neighborhood. This was the Federal Triangle, one of Washington's busiest downtown areas.

R wondered what book the sculptor had in mind when he put that one in Ben's right hand. Why were those other three on the ground—the top of the base of the pedestal—by Ben's right foot? What's the message, the symbolism? That Ben was a man of the written word? That books were important to him—to who and what he was?

Fine. Yes. That must be it.

R was suddenly aware of a putrid odor coming from his right. It had the fragrance of spoiled food, dead animals, urine, garbage— human body stench.

He dared to look in the direction of the smell. There was a man standing there, barely two feet away. He was also looking up at Ben. He appeared as filthy as he smelled. He was wearing a dark-blue knit hat full of holes, a parka that once must have been olive drab but was now covered with dark and varied stains. His trousers, baggy and brown, were folded up several times at the cuff. His white and blue sneakers were cracked and dirty. He wore no socks, his ankles were black. How old was he? It was hard to tell. His hair seemed red; so did his beard.

"Did you know that Dr. Franklin was the first person on earth to notice there was a Gulf Stream in the Atlantic Ocean?" the man asked.

R nodded.

"Did you know that Dr. Franklin, not Thomas Jefferson, came up with 'We hold these truths to be self-evident' in the Declaration of Independence?"

Again, R moved his head up and down.

"Dr. Franklin also invented the armonica, a beautiful instrument for making the most beautiful music," the man said to R. Each now turned to face the other.

The guy was definitely Caucasian but the once-white skin of his forehead and cheeks was stained with streaks of what appeared to be a combination of grease and common dirt. How long, dear God, had it been since this man had been anywhere close to running water, to soap, to being clean?

He was between fifty-five and sixty-five years old. That was R's guess after seeing his face. There was no way to tell more precisely.

"Yes," R answered. He saw no need to tell the man that he had actually played an armonica one afternoon—very much in private—at the Franklin Institute in Philadelphia.

"He took the little boy's trick of rubbing a wet finger around the rim of a water glass to make music and turned it into an instrument," said the man.

R nodded, breathing only through his mouth.

"Both Mozart *and* Beethoven wrote pieces for Dr. Franklin's armonica," said the man. "Did you know that?"

Yes, yes, R definitely knew that too. He had been so taken aback by the man's odor and appearance, he only now focused on the voice and the manner of speech. This was an astonishingly well-spoken, articulate person. What in hell was his story? Where did he come from, how did he end up like this? Could he be a disgraced or retired historian of the American Revolution scraping along by teaching on the streets? Move over, buddy, I may be joining you soon.

"He was also an expert at chess," the man, whatever he was, continued. "He wrote an essay about it that is full of wisdom—and more than chess."

R was most familiar with that essay. He particularly remembered the opening words: "The Game of Chess is not merely an idle amusement; several very valuable qualities of the mind, useful in the court of human life, are to be acquired and strengthened by it."

The smelly man said, "I have always been particularly taken by what he said in the essay about getting out of difficult situations."

.   .   .

R didn't run the thirty-five blocks back to his house in Georgetown, but he walked as fast as he probably ever had in his life.

It seemed like only a blur of minutes before he was in the library with Ben's 1,200-word essay on chess before him.

The apt phrases leaped out at him.

> If you have incautiously put yourself into a bad and dangerous position . . . you must abide by all consequences of your rashness.
>
> One so frequently, after contemplation, discovers the means of extricating one's self from a supposed insurmountable difficulty.

The most wrenchingly relevant one was:

> No false move should ever be made to extricate yourself
> out of a difficulty or to gain advantage; for there can be no
> pleasure in playing with a man once detected in such un-
> fair practice.

R went immediately to his desk. The words of confession came careening out of his mind into his fingers onto the computer keys like heat-seeking rockets. Never had he written so fast, so emotionally, so furiously.

It was ninety minutes before he stopped for a break.

By then he had, in rough note form, recounted how he had burned the Eastville papers and lied to Wes Braxton.

After going to the bathroom and gulping down a bottle of sparkling water, he tried to re-create the situation and recount every detail he could remember from the burned-up papers. But he also made the point as strongly as he could that he still was not convinced that Benjamin Franklin did, in fact, trigger two murders, especially that of the woman who bore him an illegitimate son while she herself was a child. The whole thing could be a cleverly perpetrated hoax. His own sin was that by destroying the Eastville papers he had made pursuing the truth more difficult. But it still had to be done. History demanded it. Benjamin Franklin's reputation, no matter the truth of the murder accusations, would survive because his accomplishments would ensure his proper and permanent place in history. Tricentennial planners and other Ben lovers could relax.

His points came out in a steady flow, because R was doing exactly what he knew he had to do. He was dealing with what Ben the Essayist called "the consequences of [his] rashness." He was implementing what Ben the Ghost might have labeled, in upper case, a second, even more important choice of Honor.

He was writing a statement of confession—but for what purpose? To send to a magazine, to put in a press release? To read aloud at high noon in front of Ben's statue? A book? Could it even end up being the beginning of a book? One thing at a time. Whatever, he was surely writing a long-form suicide note, because once this was read both within his profession and by the outside world, he would be dead. His reputation, his very being as a man of history, scholarship, and principle would be no more.

He too would be ashes, impossible ever to be re-formed into anything of value.

So be it. In the parlance of *Law & Order,* he was ready to do the time, even if it meant dirty clothes, no baths, and hanging out near statues of Ben.

His only pleasure was deciding that, if there ever was a book, he would send the finished manuscript to Johnny Rutledge at BFU Press rather than to Harry Dickinson. Eat your heart out, Harry!

R had a further whiff of fun when he thought about using Harry's suggestion, *Ben Three,* as the title anyhow.

All foolish flights of fancy came crashing down once he focused on the fact that he had to make a real confession directly to Wes Braxton, the sooner the better.

And there was still—also the sooner the better, probably— another confession he had to make.

And he had to go to Williamsburg in the morning.

FOURTEEN

R waited until he was thirty minutes out of Washington on I-95 South on the road to Williamsburg. Then, with great reluctance and dread, he dialed the number for the Eastern Pennsylvania Museum of Colonial History in Eastville.

He could put it off no longer.

Wes Braxton answered. It jarred R at first, because he had been unconsciously hoping, like the schoolboy waiting to see the principal, for a few more seconds of time before he had to confess his terrible sins. But, of course, acting directors of small museums have no secretaries, no assistants to answer the telephone for them.

R simply began talking to Wes. He had not worked out exactly how he was going to tell his story because he could not bear to relive what he had done any more times than absolutely necessary. The words, unprepared and unpracticed, just came.

"Wes, I'm sorry to say that I have been guilty of a serious breach of professional ethics. Those papers from the cloak may have been much more important than either Wally or I said. It's not certain, but they may very well have contained an account of a historically important and dramatically significant meeting among some of our Founding Fathers—"

"I know that. Dr. Taylor. I know."

At first, R. wasn't sure he had heard Wes's interruption correctly. "You know? You know *what,* Wes?"

"What you just said. That they could be very important."

"So . . . well, I'm a bit confused."

"I spent some time researching those scattered words and phrases even before I called Dr. Rush," said Wes. "I wasn't able to decipher them completely but there was enough there for me to pick up a real smell—of malfeasance on the part of Benjamin Franklin and of some authenticity."

R was trying to keep his cell phone at his ear with his right hand, guide his car around three trucks in the slow lane with his left, and at the same time come to grips with what he was hearing.

"Are you still there, Dr. Taylor?" Wes said finally.

"Right, you bet," said R. "I'm on a cell phone in the middle of traffic on I-Ninety-five at the moment."

"I know why you and Dr. Rush did what you did, if that's your concern."

R was now past the trucks and again reasonably clear in the heavy traffic, but he decided to remain silent anyhow. This kid, clearly even smarter and more clever than R had first noted, was in no need of any unnecessary prompting.

"Both of you were interested in protecting the reputation of the great Benjamin Franklin. I assumed that about Dr. Rush, and you pretty much said as much when you brought up the Prophecy. You really do have to be vigilant against hoaxers and debunkers. That is as much the mission of serious historians like you and Dr. Rush as finding, revealing, and analyzing new information and insights."

Wes paused. R had to say something now. "I appreciate your understanding," was what he said.

Then he sucked in his breath and confessed.

"The worst thing is that the papers—the originals I purchased from you—are no longer available for anybody to do any further research on or about. I did a most foolish, stupid, and unforgivable thing—"

"Please, please, Dr. Taylor. There is nothing to forgive."

Again R's sense of self-preservation, his desire to avoid the principal's punishment as long as possible, caused him to shut up.

"I thought it might be possible you would find a buyer for the papers that would take them out of circulation or out of access to future scholars," Wes said, "so I took the precaution of making several very clear high-definition copies. I have them locked up in our safe. They will always be available—to you or to anybody else who comes along: tomorrow, next week, next year, or next century—to pursue the accuracy of the story they tell."

R almost rammed a gray Toyota SUV in front of him. He swerved to the right to avoid rear-ending the vehicle and its passenger load of what looked to be five or six small kids. There was a rest area ahead; he quickly exited.

"Dr. Taylor, did you hear me? Boy, cell phones still are not as reliable as they should be."

"I hear you, Wes. I have pulled off and parked."

"I hate driving on I-Ninety-five. The police, for reasons that escape me, have yet to figure out how to keep all those trucks from traveling so fast and so recklessly."

R chose to leave the subject of dangerous trucks on I-95 for a future conversation. "What about being able to do further work to determine the age and authenticity of the paper and the ink?" he asked. "That certainly can't be done from copies."

"Well, sir, I'm pretty sure about the dating. Several months ago some friends and former colleagues in the documents section at Colonial Williamsburg did a complete workup for me as a favor. I have their report, also in the safe."

"For the record . . . what does it say exactly?"

"There's a seventy-five to ninety percent chance the paper was manufactured in the eighteenth century, a sixty to eighty percent chance on the ink."

R had no more questions. Nothing more to say to the principal.

Wes went on. "So, like I said, not only do you not have anything to regret or apologize for, Dr. Taylor, you have my gratitude."

Gratitude? R didn't say a word. He waited.

"I was appointed the real director of the museum last week. I was the unanimous choice of the search committee, thanks to you, sir."

Thanks to *me?*

"It was the twenty-one thousand dollars you got for the papers that did it. I will always be in your debt, Dr. Taylor."

R turned the key in the ignition of his car. "I'm glad I could help," he said.

"Where are you driving now, if I may ask?"

"To Williamsburg, as a matter of fact, for a meeting."

"That is a wonderful place for people like you and me and everyone else who appreciates the eighteenth century."

R said he agreed with Wes.

"Have a great time, sir."

R said he would certainly try.

.   .   .

They were in a chapel-like conference room in William and Mary's 300-year-old Wren Building, supposedly designed by Sir Christopher Wren, the great British architect.

R would not have been surprised if a man in a long coat and breeches had banged an ornamental mace against the floor and loudly proclaimed: "Here ye! Here ye! Here ye! This proceeding in the matter of the Good People of History versus Bad Rebecca

Kendall Lee is now in session! God save the United States of America and the American Revolution Historical Association!

But John Gwinnett offered no official call to order. He simply laid papers—the goods—out in front of Rebecca much like a dealer putting cards out for a game of blackjack.

"Here are the official results of our investigation, Dr. Lee," he said. "This, of course, is the same material that we forwarded to you earlier."

With the smack of paper on the long polished table came the message: *Here now, You Cursed Accused, is the evidence against you.*

"I have read it all, thank you," said Rebecca.

Gwinnett might have been expecting her to be intimidated by the setting he had created for this confrontation. If so, it wasn't working. There was nothing here she couldn't handle, her body language announced.

"This does not add up to plagiarism," she said, without looking at the papers.

She and Gwinnett were seated across the table from each other. Sonya Lyman and Joe Hooper were on Gwinnett's left, R on his right.

"I most assuredly think it does," said Gwinnett, as calm and self-assured as Rebecca.

Officials at William and Mary called the Wren Building the *soul of the college* because of its age and its location at the west end of Duke of Gloucester, the main pedestrian street that runs the length of Colonial Williamsburg's historic area. R had observed the eighteenth-century furniture and the large portraits of past William and Mary presidents and Colonial Virginia dignitaries, but only now did he note the smell of antiquity that filled the room. He had a sense that even the air in this place was old and preserved. The atmosphere, obviously as Gwinnett planned, oozed history, importance, gravitas.

Here now, in the presence of the great Patrick Henry himself, were serious people gathered to consider serious business.

Yes, Patrick Henry, alias Alexander Stockton, Gwinnett's chief assistant, was the sixth person in the room. He was all dressed up in white knee socks and lace collar, tight green breeches, and a long dark-brown coat with gold buttons down the front.

"You can see why we call him Patrick," Gwinnett had said in introducing Stockton, who would take notes of the meeting. "He is an accomplished actor, so as an escape from his serious work for me and the college he regularly plays Patrick Henry for Colonial Williamsburg events. He has such a date later in the day, so I said it was fine for him to come here as a properly clothed and ready Patrick."

R had seen many oil portraits and sketches of the famous Virginia radical, the man who created the revolution's major battle cry, "Give me liberty or give me death." Stockton, in his late thirties, definitely bore a resemblance, with a similar sharp nose and facial features and an unwigged head of long curled dark-brown hair worn down his back in a ponytail. Of course they called him Patrick.

"We have gathered here for you to present whatever evidence you may wish in your defense," Gwinnett said to Rebecca.

"*We,* a jury of my peers?"

"I would say we're only at the *grand* jury phase right now," interjected Hooper.

After an annoyed I'm-in-charge-here glance at Hooper, Gwinnett said to Rebecca, "Terminology aside, our preliminary finding is that you have committed plagiarism, the writer's most mortal sin. Do I not speak for us all?"

Gwinnett then turned first to R, then Sonya. Both nodded in agreement. Joe held up his right hand: *Not yet, not until I've heard the defense,* was the message.

"Thank you, Dr. Hooper," said Rebecca. "I am delighted to

find at least one open mind in this lynch mob—sorry; on this distinguished ARHA committee."

Rebecca had yet to make real eye contact with Gwinnett, Sonya Lyman, or Joe Hooper. She had given a stunned and then amused look at Stockton as Patrick Henry, but only R had had the benefit of a direct stare. That came in a whisk when she entered the room, silently and with no mutual acknowledgments. Hers was a look of comfort. If she was afraid, you couldn't read it in her eyes.

R saw John Gwinnett's calmness as just as unusual, considering the potentially explosive nature of this event for him as well. Maybe the presence of Patrick Henry raised the comfort level.

R himself was neither calm nor comfortable. He had spent most of the two hours of his post-Braxton drive sorting through concerns about most everything that had already happened to him and that would—could, even should—happen now.

"Maybe this distinguished committee would like to observe a demonstration of what I think of this evidence against me?" Rebecca asked.

It was not a real question.

In a stunningly swift and deft series of moves, she reached out and grabbed the documents from the table, stood up with them held before her like they were smelly garbage, took five long fast steps, and crashed the papers down into a large leather eighteenth-century trash receptacle to her right.

"Now I'm ready for your questions," Rebecca declared, her legs slightly apart, her hands on her hips. At that moment, she could have passed for an attack dog at a breached security checkpoint.

R, without consciously doing so, was on his feet. It had been a reactive move. Joe and Sonya remained seated, along with Gwinnett, the man with a new right knee, and his costumed assistant, Alexander Stockton.

Seconds clicked by. Soon this still life had to end. Somebody was going to have to say or do something.

R acted first. "Sit down, Rebecca." The words came out of his mouth like a spontaneous bark, an uncontrolled air horn. "Now!" he shouted, when Rebecca didn't immediately move.

She blanched. She actually moved her head backward as if she had been hit by something. The comfort was gone from her eyes, but it was replaced more by wonder than by fear.

R had no idea how the others were reacting. He kept his eyes on Rebecca Kendall Lee, the Cursed Accused.

He sat back down. In silence, Rebecca slowly returned to her seat across from Gwinnett. She lowered her head and did not look at R or at anybody else.

His voice low, uncharged, almost friendly, R said, "Rebecca, those papers you just trashed contain iron-clad proof of blatant acts of plagiarism on a massive scale in your Reagan book. As you know, there were more than seventy instances of *direct* copying of material and another hundred or so that range from *nearly identical* or *similar* to *indirect*. I began to wonder, frankly, if there's an original line or idea in the whole damn book."

Her head shot up. "I don't give a damn about what you wonder, R."

"You are a disgrace!" Gwinnett said. "You are a criminal as common as the lowest thug on the streets . . ."

He didn't finish his sentence but stopped talking and watched, along with the others, as Rebecca pulled several sheets of paper from a small briefcase and threw them down on the table, one at a time, in front of each of them, beginning with Gwinnett.

"Lectures about plagiarism I do not take from you, O Distinguished Patrick Henry Historian-slash-Scholar," she said to Gwinnett. "Read it and weep. Your faux Patrick Henry there beside you can wipe your eyes."

R knew something like this was coming; it was inevitable. But now that she had actually counterattacked John Gwinnett, an even stronger rush of anger toward Rebecca began to rise within him.

Gwinnett was laughing. *Laughing!* Harry Dickinson had said the man had laughed inexplicably when told of Rebecca's coming attempt to blackmail him. Maybe there was something wrong with his mind as well as his right knee. Stockton was also laughing. Whatever the joke was, he was in on it too.

Now Gwinnett, still chuckling, slid the paper back across the table at Rebecca. "Whatever weeping I do, Dr. Lee, will be from having been brought to tears by uncontrollable merriment. I may laugh until I cry, but there is nothing on that paper to trigger any other emotion."

"It proves you committed plagiarism," said a defiant if obviously confused Rebecca. "You stole word for word what that other guy wrote, the same thing you accuse me of doing. I warned you, all of you. Let he—or she—who is without sin cast the first stone."

The room was absolutely silent. Even the antiquated eighteenth-century air wasn't moving.

With a huge smile still on his face, John Gwinnett reached his right hand, palm up, across and in front of Stockton.

On cue, Stockton handed Gwinnett a smooth white stone the size and shape of a large lemon drop.

Gwinnett scooted it across the table to Rebecca. The stone stopped perfectly, four or five inches from her. R was reminded of the coin ceremony at Christ Church Burial Ground for Wally.

Rebecca looked down at the stone as if it were radioactive.

"Dr. Lee, I have news for you that is going to cause you great disappointment," said Gwinnett.

She was listening—and staring. So were R and the others. Stockton, however, was smiling in anticipation of what was to come.

"The John Gwinnett who wrote that piece thirty-seven years ago for the Emory University historical review called *Southern Perspective* was not me, Dr. Lee. Strange as it might seem to you, there were, at that time, two John Gwinnetts in the field of early American history: John P. Gwinnett and John T. Gwinnett. We were not related. I am the P. The other, the T., was a specialist in tobacco farming in the early colonies who died fourteen years ago after suffering a heart attack while lecturing at a small college in southeast Oklahoma. Or maybe it was central Kansas—or northern Nebraska maybe? One of those places out there, was it not, Stockton?"

"Yes, sir," said Stockton. "It was, in fact, Emporia State College in Emporia, Kansas, in the central part of the state."

R, acting spontaneously, clapped his hands together a couple of times. Sonya joined him. So did Joe Hooper a few seconds later.

"All right," said Rebecca. "You got me."

Rebecca Kendall Lee, defiant attacker, was suddenly no more. Her face, tense and on edge before, had fallen. She put her elbows on the table and thrust her head down into her hands.

"Go ahead, ruin me," she said, in a near whisper.

"You ruined yourself, Dr. Lee," said Gwinnett, in a voice reminiscent of a lecturing criminal court judge on television. "We reap what we sow—"

R interrupted. "Rebecca, it's time to help yourself. Are there any mitigating circumstances that you believe we should know about?"

She dropped her hands and looked over at him. "I got too busy, R, that's it, pure and simple. I decided I could have it all: give lectures from one end of the country to the other, appear on all the television networks, and still write my articles and books. When time and schedules got tighter and tighter, something had to give. Nobody could fill in for me on the lecture circuit or the TV gigs but they could do my books, so that's what happened. I hired a team of researchers and writers, made them sign unto-death confidentiality agreements, and put them to work writing my stuff."

R thought he saw tears forming in her eyes. In all the years he had known Rebecca, he could not recall a time when she had cried. Many of the men he was around at BFU, including Wally, teared up more than she did. It was truly a serious moment in this woman's life.

"So, to put it directly, you are admitting to the crime—offense, whatever—of plagiarism?" It was Joe Hooper.

"It is indeed a crime in most states of the union," said Gwinnett. "I had Stockton check. It's been a while since anyone has been formally charged or sent to jail, but it is a misdemeanor in thirty-five states—including Virginia."

Rebecca stood and put her hands in front of her. "Cuff me and read me my rights. I throw myself on the mercy of the court."

R motioned for her to sit down and cool it. He really was trying to help her, if she would let him. Continuing his dramatic mood swing, he was feeling some sympathy—and mercy—for Rebecca. She had been a brilliant student and an honorable member of the Ben Crowd before branching out to do her own thing.

Rebecca, defeated, took her seat again. "Yes, Dr. Hooper, I am guilty, not of direct premeditated plagiarism but of something equally awful. My only defense is that I did not pay close enough attention to what my researchers and writers were doing. I didn't consciously decide to steal certain lines, paragraphs, ideas, and themes from other authors. My staff—sometimes toward the end of getting the book done there were five or six of them—simply didn't bother to transform other people's work into different words for me, and I was too busy to pay attention to what they were doing."

"What about the book galleys?" Joe Hooper asked. "Why didn't you catch it once it was set in type?"

"I was traveling when the galleys came to my office. The publisher wanted them back in a week. I had somebody on the staff do the proofreading. I never looked at them."

"This is outrageous, inexcusable, and monstrous," Gwinnett said.

"I know it, OK?" Rebecca stiffened again. Her face came back to life. "So I guess this means no mercy—no act of forgiveness—is possible?"

Gwinnett turned to Stockton. "Patrick, what was it you said in your Christian Forgiveness speech?"

Stockton laid down the ballpoint pen with which he was taking notes at one end of the table. He straightened himself in his chair and said, in a voice clearly designed to sound like Patrick Henry, " 'Our mild and holy system of religion inculcates an admirable maxim of forbearance. If your enemy smite one cheek, turn the other to him. But you must stop there. You cannot apply this to your country. As members of a social community, this maxim does not apply to you.' "

Gwinnett, turning back to Rebecca, added, "I think it goes without saying that we, the members of this committee, are functioning as members of the social community, not as individuals."

"So ye shall smite me, is that it?" said Rebecca. "Well, say I, smite me in the courts of law or public opinion, and I guarantee there will be returning smites that you—none of you—will enjoy."

Oh, God, thought R. Here she goes again. He wanted to yell at Gwinnett to calm down, be a good winner. It was his turn to cool it.

But that was not to be.

"You have more criminality up your sleazy sleeve?" Gwinnett said in a snarl that was most unlike a Virginia gentleman.

Rebecca was back on her feet. "As a matter of fact, I do have one more shot in my gun, one more arrow in my quiver—one I had about decided I would not deploy."

She turned toward R.

"I'm sorry, R, but I have no choice. If you and your fellow mob members move against me, I will be ruined. I will become the disgraced historian, permanently scarred by the scarlet letter *P* for Plagiarist on my forehead. There will be no more book or magazine contracts, no more lectures, no more television appearances—no more good life as a public historian-cum-commentator. *I* will be history. So please understand what I must do is not personal about you and Wally. It's personal about me. It's you and Wally or it's me. I have chosen to survive."

R was struck by only one irrational thought: Where was that lethal statuette of Ben when he really needed it?

Rebecca stepped away from the table and, much as she had done at the first Cosmos Club meeting, prepared to make a rehearsed address. She even cleared her throat.

"I hereby charge, as God and R are my witnesses, that the late Wally Rush and the present R Taylor conspired together to commit one of the largest literary hoaxes of its kind ever perpetrated. There is strong circumstantial evidence that these two distinguished men of American history and letters—"

R rose.

"Stop it, Rebecca!" The words came out in a cold shout, as if directed to an unruly crowd at the other end of a football field.

Now, with the help of Stockton and a cane, John Gwinnett got to his feet. So did Sonya and Joe. R saw it as their way of rising to what was clearly going to be an occasion.

"What's this all about, Dr. Taylor, if I may ask?" Gwinnett said.

Rebecca didn't let him answer. "It's about the fact that I believe and can convince anyone that R wrote *Ben Two* for Wally Rush." she said. "You can't call it plagiarism, but it may be something even more wrong: fraud, possibly? Fraud on the American public, on the Pulitzer Prize committee, on the worlds of American history and letters. If what I did was a misdemeanor, what they did was—is—a felony, may I say, of the highest order."

She returned to the table for her briefcase and purse, headed for the door, and turned dramatically. "Go public with your charges against me, and I will go public with mine about *Ben Two*. The choice is yours—and so are the consequences."

Her words had an instant paralyzing effect—on her and on the others. She went motionless instead of rushing on to finish her dramatic exit. Everyone else was quiet too.

"Is it true that you wrote Wally Rush's book?" John Gwinnett asked R, finally fracturing the stillness.

FIFTEEN

A telephone call from Harry Dickinson had actually started the whole thing.

"Every morning I wait with a glow of high anticipation about what the man from FedEx has brought me from Gray House in Philadelphia," Harry had said to R. "And every morning I am disappointed."

"I'll put Wally on the phone. He's still upstairs."

"In a minute, R, in a minute. First, *you* tell me how he's doing on the masterpiece."

R had so wanted to believe Wally was working hard on *Ben Two* on his own, late at night or on weekends, and simply had failed to mention it. But that was a delusion. Wally did everything, including his writing, in full view and sound of most everyone—particularly R, his most trusted aide and helper. "My right arm, leg, and brain" was what Wally called him.

Until now, until Harry pressed the point, R had tried to ignore both the obvious and his accompanying concern about Wally, his employer, friend, mentor—hero.

"I'm sure it's coming along just fine," R said to Harry as

smoothly as he could manage. "He simply doesn't want to talk about it right now."

"Where I come from, they would say your response has the texture and fragrance of pure fantasy," said Harry.

When Harry Dickinson spoke of "where I come from," he meant mostly Harvard and the West Side of Manhattan after a childhood in Baltimore.

R had made no reply to Harry's put-down of his speculation about Wally. He just transferred the call to Wally's extension in the second-floor master bedroom. R had left Wally there a hour ago, still in bed reading *The Inquirer*. On some mornings now, even after R arrived for work, Wally spent nearly two hours reading the paper. R had begun to wonder if Wally was meticulously going through the classified ads as well as the news stories. . . .

"Harry says he's coming down here a week from tomorrow to personally pick up whatever I have done on *Ben Two*."

Wally was standing in the doorway of the library. Obviously, the call from Harry had been completed. R noticed for the first time that Wally's torso, still covered in pajamas and a robe, was broadening and his hair was still gray but it needed a cut. It was down over his ears already. Earlier, R had observed that Wally had begun to flatten the pattern and inflections of his words, but R had not yet made the connection with any of this to Ben. Wally was already seventy-five, so R had attributed the speech, the heft and the hair, as well as his growing lack of energy and mental acuity, simply to part of the aging process. Seeing Wally every day as he did, R had not added up the symptoms of Wally's morphing into Ben—not yet.

"What *have* you written on *Ben Two*, Wally?" R asked.

"Only the title page." Before R could get out a response, Wally added, "Will you help me, R? I can't write the book. I want to, I'm desperate to, but I can't. Help me, please."

"Of course," R said, without a split second of thought—or doubt.

There could be no other answer. Wally Rush was the man who had taken R's love of early American history, triggered first by a marvelous high school teacher and two undergraduate professors, and transformed it into a profession, a way of life.

R—then "Ray" to one and all—had entered high school in Griswold, Connecticut, as a left-handed football quarterback and baseball pitcher, a student body leader who seemed headed nowhere in particular afterward. He graduated with academic as well as athletic honors with his mind aglow about history because of Olivia Huntington. She was a tiny, shy, single Briton who had fallen in love with the Berkshires as a tourist and gone back there to live after retiring from a thirty-two-year career as a curator at the National Portrait Gallery in London. The Griswold schools jumped at the chance to have her teach history, something she did with a quiet gusto that switched on in R a passionate curiosity about the past. With her help, he got a full academic scholarship to Wesleyan University in Middletown, a quality small school in southern Connecticut. That was where he met Wally, who came to lecture one evening on "Benjamin Franklin, the First American." R was captured, not only by Wally but also by Ben, and decided that evening that he would do his graduate work at BFU. Again, he did so on full academic scholarship and a job as Wally's graduate assistant. That led to an MA, a Ph.D., a decision to be called R rather than Ray or Raymond, and appointment as assistant professor of history and Wally's chief assistant.

R spent the rest of the day and all night going through Wally's outline for *Ben Two* and the notes and sources that had been gathered for each potential chapter and section. R knew the basic material because he had been in charge of the three-person research team hired to assemble the material for Wally.

It wasn't until early afternoon the next day that the real work began. R had taken a four-hour break to return to his own apartment for a quick nap, a shower, and some clean clothes.

Then he went back to Gray House, sat down before the empty screen of Wally's desktop computer in the study, and typed PART ONE—THE LONDON YEARS.

There were no security problems because the four other people who worked full-time directly for Wally—a secretary and three graduate assistants, including Rebecca Lee at the time—stayed at Wally's departmental offices on the BFU campus. Only R and Wally knew what was going on at Gray House.

R stayed at the computer all that night and remained there, with only occasional breaks for food and brief naps, for the next week, each day ending with his submitting what had been written to Wally for approval. Wally, as engaged as it was possible for him to be, always had some edits and suggestions—most of them helpful and constructive.

Harry History Channel showed up on the eighth day as he had promised, coming down on the train from New York to retrieve whatever had been done.

The manuscript delivery was made over a jolly lunch of rare roast beef, lobster bisque, small wheat wafers, and a French cabernet sauvignon at Café William, a musty twenty-table place two blocks from Wally's house, where he routinely ate either lunch or dinner half a dozen times a week.

The occasion was jolly because there were 125 double-spaced manuscript pages in the manila envelope Wally handed to Harry as the three men sat down. R was as comfortable at Café William as Wally. It was decorated casually in what passed for Old Philadelphia Tavern style. The china and the silverware, as well as the food and drink, were heavy. The walls were covered with a mix of drawings and prints of people and events from eighteenth-century Philadelphia, including several of Ben.

Harry, before looking at a menu or putting a napkin in his lap, whipped the pages out of the envelope and began reading.

R remembered precisely what Harry said as he read the first two pages.

"Good . . . really good . . . nice . . . really nice. Terrific beginning."

Then R, who was sitting opposite Harry, watched the famous editor from New York skip ahead ten or fifteen pages. He read two, three, four more consecutive pages.

"Well done . . . yes . . . that works."

Harry continued to move through twenty or so pages at a time, reading and then proclaiming or mumbling his pleasure with what he saw.

Finally, he tapped the pages against the table a few times to even them out and replaced the heavy rubber band around the manuscript.

"It's one helluva beginning," he announced to Wally. There was a slight trace of a smile on his face. "Frankly, I'm surprised— most pleasantly so."

Neither Wally nor R said anything. This was definitely Harry's show.

"I didn't believe you had done a damned thing on the book, to tell you the absolute truth," he said to Wally. "On *Ben One,* you couldn't wait to get me something to look at. This time, silence. I had assumed that nothing meant there *was* nothing. My apologies, Wally, for my rank suspicions and awful thoughts about you. I was beginning to work on the manner and timing of asking for the return of your advance."

"Accepted," Wally said quickly, and motioned for the waiter to come take their orders.

"When can I expect another delivery?" Harry asked.

"That depends," said Wally, looking directly at R through the black horn-rim glasses he was still wearing back then.

"Three ... maybe four months?" said R to Wally. "At the rate you're going, that would be my estimate. What do *you* think?"

Wally grinned and looked back at Harry. "Three, maybe four months. Right."

They sealed the promise by clinking and then emptying their wineglasses. And it was on with lunch.

It was also on with *Ben Two*.

The next 135 pages were delivered to Harry in New York via FedEx three and a half months later.

That prompted a call to R from Harry.

"It's his best work yet," said Harry. "The writing's superb, and so are the narrative drive and the organization."

R said, "Thank you. On behalf of Wally, thank you."

"I didn't know he had it in him, to be honest. It's such a glory and a pleasure to read this stuff. It really does sing, in a way—well, in a way far superior to anything in *Ben One,* I must say. I don't have to tell you that this is exactly what happened to Ben himself. His prose, like Wally's, ripened and blossomed with age."

R did not have to be told that. Ben went from a composer of heavy-handed political tracts to an elegant wordsmith whose writings were among the very best of his time. Among the Founding Fathers, possibly only Thomas Paine in *Common Sense* could be said to have turned a better phrase than Ben. Not Jefferson and certainly not Adams or even Madison. And Washington, of course, wrote with a thud that matched his personality.

"If we publish it well and—I promise you we will—and get a few major reviewer breaks, we might really get that Pulitzer this time," said Harry. "We could send Wally out on a book tour. He really is beginning to act a bit like Ben, isn't he? That long hair, the developing paunch, the speaking manner. When he replaces those horn-rims with wire specs we'll know he's a goner. Maybe that's what's helping him write so magnificently about Ben, who knows? Who cares? Whatever, he's writing a masterpiece."

R hadn't yet fully focused on Wally's Ben transformations. Right then his mind was stuck on what Harry had said about the masterpiece and the Pulitzer possibilities for *Ben Two*.

Then Harry, clearly having realized the dangers in what he had said, came back to add, "For God's sake, don't quote me on that possible Pulitzer to Wally. I don't want to raise his hopes again." And R promised not to breathe a word.

In fact, he and Wally exchanged few words over the next months about anything other than the book itself. R kept writing as fast and well as he could, involving Wally in the process as reader, editor, and consultant. R would take a stack of finished manuscript, thirty or forty pages at a time, for Wally to read; Wally always ended each reading with a quiet "Thank you, R" or "Well, done, my friend."

R continued to send off the completed sections to Harry, usually in 125- or 150-page hunks, each received with increasingly ecstatic rave notices.

The drain on R's physical and intellectual energy was enormous. On the day he actually typed THE END on the last page of what ended up being a 535-page manuscript, not counting footnotes and bibliography, the emotional toll also kicked in.

Following the pattern, he sat at the desk in the Gray House library while Wally, having been summoned by R, sat on the other side, reading the final words R had written for him.

Strange as it might seem, R did not want to smack his hero Wally Rush across the face, scream "You're pure bullshit!" at him, grab the manuscript from him and throw it in the fireplace, or race with it to a third-floor window and toss it to the Philadelphia winds. To yell "*I* wrote this, not *you!*"; to sob; to laugh hysterically.

"You have written a magnificent book, R," Wally said.

"We did it together, Wally," R replied.

"Thank you, but what you have given me is the ultimate gift. You have given me your talent, your intellect, your creative being. I can never thank you adequately, I know that. But I can do one thing—whatever financial rewards come from this book will be shared by us equally. I will instruct Harry to automatically divide all royalties half and half."

Wally pulled something from his pocket and tossed it across the desk. "This is a check for one hundred and thirty thousand dollars—half the advance Harry paid me for *Ben Two.*"

R's family were small-town New Englanders; his father was a minister, his mother was a homemaker and volunteer. Checks for this much money were not part of his life, either growing up or as a historian and professor. *Franklin at Craven Street* had sold barely 7,000 copies on a $3,500 advance; *Ben and Billy,* only slightly more.

The check lay there between Wally and R, who made no effort to take it.

"You must, R. If you don't, then—well, I don't know what I'll do."

R was hit by a consuming, shuddering sense of sadness and love for his friend. This wonderful human being was disintegrating as he lost both his mental faculties and his sense of himself.

"It's a deal," R said, taking the check.

Wally got up from his chair and came around to the other side. The author and his collaborator embraced, one of only a few times they had ever done so in the years they had been friends and associates.

Harry kept his word. Green Tree published the book more than well. There were full-page ads in *The New York Times Book Review* and *The Washington Post Book World* and smaller ones in *The New Yorker, Newsweek,* and *Time.* They sent Wally out on a book tour and talk-show rounds in New York, Chicago, Boston, San Francisco, and Seattle. *Ben Two* went almost immediately to number 1 on both the Amazon.com and Barnes and Noble nonfiction lists and within three weeks began a long stint in the top five on the *New York Times, Washington Post, Wall Street Journal, Publishers Weekly,* and most other best-seller lists. There were second, third, and fourth printings that put nearly 400,000 hardback copies of the book in print. Paperback rights sold at auction for $350,000. International sales flooded in, as did Hollywood movie and PBS-type documentary interest.

As expected, *Ben Two* was named a finalist in the Pulitzer biography category.

Wally and R were sitting on either side of the partners' desk on the April afternoon the winners were to be announced. Harry, having come down from New York with his confidence about victory raging way beyond perfunctory, was sitting at one end of the desk in a pulled-up chair. He had ordered a case of expensive champagne that was on ice in the kitchen and had a person in his office back in New York standing by at a computer to read the Associated Press wire. Nobody got an official telephone call telling them about winning a Pulitzer. It was announced by the people at Columbia University to the press first.

At three-fifteen the phone rang. The one thing they had not specifically worked out among the three of them was who would actually answer the telephone.

On the second ring, Harry picked it up. "Yes?" he said.

He listened for a few seconds, stood, raised his right arm high over his head, and said, "We did it!" Then to Wally, he said, "Congratulations, Dr. Pulitzer Prize Winner."

Within minutes, the champagne was flowing and the house was filling with students—including Rebecca, R now remembered—professors, and other friends.

After a while somebody began yelling, "Speech! Speech!"

A library ladder was pulled out for Wally to stand on. The people crowded in the library—and spilling out into the hallways and parlor and dining room—went silent and gathered around as best they could.

Before Wally could say anything, a kid started everybody singing:

> "For he's a Wally good fellow,
> For he's a Wally good fellow,
> For he's a Wally good fe-ello,
> That nobody can deny."

Then Jackson Hall, the BFU provost, raised his glass of champagne and yelled, "To Wally!"

"To Wally!" repeated the crowd.

Once things got more or less quiet, Wally spoke.

"Thank you, Jackson. Thank you, one and all. As all of you know, no book is ever really the work of one person, particularly a biography like *Ben Two*. I want to thank several of you in this room—these rooms, I guess I should say—tonight, who helped me, each in your own way, to bring this book into being. There are too many of you to call by name. But you know who you are—and I salute you all."

He raised his glass, as did everyone else as they said, "Hear, hear," and downed a sip of champagne.

Wally invited R to go with him to New York for the Pulitzer Awards lunch at Columbia in June. R declined.

Shortly afterward he submitted his notice to Wally and to the university. He told everyone he wanted to get more deeply into his research for his planned book on the Washington, Adams, and Jefferson presidencies—and Washington, D.C., was the place to do that.

Wally and R never spoke another word to each other about the writing of *Ben Two*.

R never spoke to anyone else either—until now.

SIXTEEN

"Yes, it's true," R said to John Gwinnett.

He looked at Rebecca, standing at the door as still as a statue.

"But it's also true that it was Wally's book. Wally's lifework went into it. I may have performed much of the physical labor at the very end, but the journey that led to its creation was taken by Wally, not by me."

Rebecca's body seemed to vibrate slightly. It was the only movement in the room. "But you do admit to having committed a hoax?" she said, in a tone that was not as strong as the words.

"I admit to you now, and I will gladly—willingly, and with some relief, frankly—admit to the world that I helped the great Wallace Stephen Rush, my late friend and mentor, transform the product of his scholarship and wisdom into a book titled *Ben Two*. I was honored to do it. There was no element of hoax involved."

Rebecca raised her hands in a halfhearted act of resignation, if not surrender. Then she said to Stockton, "Did you help *your* esteemed mentor transform *his* scholarship and wisdom about Patrick Henry into his forthcoming masterpiece? What about it, *Patrick*? Want to confess, too?"

"Leave us at once!" Gwinnett roared at Rebecca. "You are truly despicable!"

And she was gone.

In the silence that followed, Gwinnett slowly sat back down. So did Joe, Sonya, and R. Stockton had remained seated all through the endgame.

"That woman is a vile, felonious liar and swine for whom the administration of a lethal injection would be more than appropriate," said Gwinnett, pointedly avoiding R's revelation about *Ben Two*—at least for now.

Sonya, who had said little since this extraordinary meeting began, joined in. "As a longtime outspoken opponent of capital punishment, even I would gladly insert the needle."

There were ten seconds of unspoken approval.

"So, what do we do about her?" asked Joe Hooper. "I hope nobody was seriously suggesting that we prefer criminal charges."

R shook his head.

"Unfortunately not," said Gwinnett. "I would love to do so, but I think such a move would draw bees of criticism that would undermine our purposes."

"That leaves us with what?" Hooper asked. "Throwing our very small book at her?"

"We prepare a statement of findings that we forward to the ARHA with a recommendation that it take whatever actions it deems appropriate," said Gwinnett, who had clearly come prepared for this. "I think it might be wise for us, in a break with custom, to release our findings to the public simultaneously. That would, of course, enlarge the size of the book being thrown almost immediately."

When no one reacted, Gwinnett said, "I would suggest that going public would also be a fair precaution against the most likely possibility that Dr. Lee will mount vigorous campaigns of coercion against others among our ARHA colleagues to prevent final sanctions of any kind. We may very well have a serious war on our hands."

There were three nods of agreement. Yes, that was a most likely possibility. "Count on it," R said.

Once again, Gwinnett turned to Stockton. "Patrick, you spoke eloquently, more so than any other person in history, about taking a stand for what one believes."

This time Stockton stood up and moved away from the table. Then, in the mode of Patrick Henry, he forcefully orated:

" 'Gentlemen may cry, Peace, peace—but there is no peace. The war is actually begun! The next gale that sweeps from the North will bring to our ears the clash of resounding arms. Our brethren are already in the field! Why stand we here idle? What is it that gentlemen wish? What would they have? Is life so dear, or peace so sweet, as to be purchased at the price of chains and slavery? Forbid it, Almighty God! I know not what course others may take; but as for me, give me liberty or give me death!"

R couldn't recall ever hearing a more phony, inappropriate use of a historical quote. To compare the ARHA versus Rebecca Kendall Lee to the Colonial States of America versus the Crown— well, it was ridiculous.

But Gwinnett was aglow. He even applauded. "Thank you, Patrick," he said, as if he were really talking to Patrick Henry.

R saw this as a whole new wrinkle to Wally's know-him, talk-to-him mantra for historians. Gwinnett didn't have to go to some faraway place such as 36 Craven Street to speak to *his* hero. He had him right there in the office.

R had a quick vision of Gwinnett doing his research. There was Stockton at Gwinnett's side dressed in his Patrick Henry outfit. Gwinnett simply turned and said, "Patrick, when were you born?" Or, "Patrick, what was it you said about liberty and death?" "Patrick, what is your favorite food and drink?" "Patrick, who does your hair?"

Thank you, Patrick.

R amused himself further by thinking of how grateful he was that Wally chose to morph into Ben himself rather than forcing R to do so. Poor Stockton.

Poor Stockton. Could it be that Rebecca, evil as she was, might have guessed right about Stockton doing the same thing for Gwinnett that I did for Wally? No, no, no. . . .

"Before adjourning, I would like to make official what we have decided by taking a vote on this matter," said Gwinnett, unknowingly interrupting R's evil thoughts. "All in favor of proceeding against Rebecca Kendall Lee in the manner just discussed, please say Aye."

There were four Ayes.

"Thank you. I will have Patrick here—pardon me, Stockton—prepare the proper materials and statements for dispatch to all concerned at the ARHA," said John Gwinnett.

Here ye, here ye, here ye. Our business has been done. The confrontation is concluded. This meeting is over.

Not quite. One matter, one elephant-sized issue, remained—in the air rather than on the table.

It was Sonya who finally spoke of it. "What *are* you going to do about your *Ben Two* story, R?" Her words came out slowly, quietly, sympathetically.

"I'm going to have to work that out," said R. "I want to do it in a way that does not hurt Wally's reputation, his legacy. Whatever Rebecca might say, it really is his book, not mine."

"Maybe you could do a new book of your own about how you came to help Wally," said Sonya. "Tell, in some detail, the story behind the story—how you made the choices you did to assist your friend."

Oh, yes. Choices. A book about choices. It could open with Ben's rules on choices. Then segue into an analysis of his Morals of Chess essay. . . .

R had yet to figure out where the choices bit had come from. Someday he might go back through Ben's writings and other papers to see what the great man really did say on the subject—if anything. Maybe, like the "difficult situation," the words from Ben had been stored way, way back in R's mind for a while. It's also possible, of course, that only R himself was speaking about choices through Ben that day in the parlor. . . .

Joe Hooper said to R with a slight grin on his face, "The very-worst-case scenario, as I see it, is that you get some well-publicized credit for having written a best-selling book about Benjamin Franklin and maybe even a belated half of Dr. Rush's Pulitzer Prize. Write a new book well enough, and you might win another, too."

"You could call it *Ben Three,*" added Sonya, also smiling.

R did not dare return the happy smiles.

He looked instead at John Gwinnett, who said in his most serious chairman's voice, "Whatever, you have put that awful Dr. Lee in a position to do no harm—either to you or to the work of this committee and to our purposes and profession. Good man, Taylor."

Good man, Taylor.

R couldn't help but wonder what Ben might say about that.

This is JIM LEHRER's fifteenth novel. He's also the author of two memoirs and three plays and is the executive editor and anchor of *The NewsHour with Jim Lehrer* on PBS. He lives in Washington, D.C., with his novelist wife, Kate. They have three daughters.

This book was set in Bulmer, a typeface designed in the late eighteenth century by the London type-cutter William Martin. The typeface was created especially for the Shakespeare Press, directed by William Bulmer; hence, the font's name. Bulmer is considered to be a transitional typeface, containing characteristics of old-style and modern designs. It is recognized for its elegantly proportioned letters, with their long ascenders and descenders.